Penguin Crime Fiction
Code Name Hangman

Paul Geddes is a lawyer who lives in
London with his wife and two children.
He has also written *The Ottawa
Allegation*, *The High Game* and
A November Wind.

Paul Geddes

Code Name Hangman

Penguin Books

Penguin Books Ltd, Harmondsworth,
Middlesex, England
Penguin Books, 625 Madison Avenue,
New York, New York 10022, U.S.A.
Penguin Books Australia Ltd, Ringwood,
Victoria, Australia
Penguin Books Canada Ltd, 2801 John Street,
Markham, Ontario, Canada L3R 1B4
Penguin Books (N.Z.) Ltd, 182–190 Wairau Road,
Auckland 10, New Zealand

First published in Great Britain under
the title *Hangman* by Faber and Faber
Limited 1977
First published in the United States
of America under the title *Hangman*
by St Martin's Press, Inc., 1977
Published in Penguin Books under
the title *Code Name Hangman* 1979

Made and printed in Great Britain by
C. Nicholls & Company Ltd
Set in Monotype Times

For P. W.-W.

1

Suddenly across the valley, there was the landmark Seagram had been told to look for, a grey wedge of stone thrusting upwards from a velvet hill: the *donjon* of Mersac. The grass slopes below the tower gave it an abandoned appearance as though a fortress had crumbled away, leaving only the *donjon* unvanquished, a last uplifted finger of warning to the traveller.

Fifty metres down the hill on which the tower stood, the houses of Mersac clustered. Too large for a village; but he would hardly have called it a town. He could see three church spires, the façade of what might be the *mairie* and slightly apart a concrete box which announced itself as the Agricultural Co-operative. But unless there were some on the other side of the hill, there seemed less than a hundred houses.

The road swung left and narrowed for a river bridge in the valley. Seagram glanced at his watch. Three-quarters of an hour had passed since he had picked up the hire car in Cahors. As he had driven the green Renault south, the rain clouds that had enveloped his flight from Heathrow had weakened, ebbing away to the western hills. As yet he had seen no sun. But the plumes of dust behind the cars that passed him going towards Montauban were growing larger and the grass on the verges was dry and yellow. It was up there somewhere, the sun that Venniker had gone after five years ago. Seagram could smell it, in the grass, in the dust, in the plastic upholstery of the Renault. It had baked this landscape for half a summer and would be back again before the day ended.

Overshooting the fork off the N20, Seagram had been obliged to consult the Michelin map he had bought as an afterthought when the car from Scotland Yard had dropped him at the airport with half an hour to spare. But, for such a small place, Mersac was well served by minor roads and the mistake had cost him little time. Once off the highway, he had found himself in countryside so orderly and unblemished as to seem studied in its effect.

Petite culture stretched in geometric strips on either side of the valley. Every kilometre or so a stone cottage or larger house was standing guard over the vegetables. There was no sound apart from the noise of the Renault's engine, no movement other than his own. Earlier in life, certainly before he became a policeman, he might have stopped the car and gazed across this landscape to the line of stony hills on the horizon, in case the silence and the order offered answers he had not heard before. When the thought came to him, he played with it idly. But he was not yet far enough from London for fanciful games. He had lit a cigarette, bored and a little stiff. Then as the road turned and dropped to yield a different view, there had been the *donjon*.

Seagram parked the Renault in the main square, and got out. The afternoon reopening of the shops had just begun; a few people watched him – a bulky, slow-moving man with fine black hair going grey, dressed in a city suit that would have been too heavy even in Mersac's spring. He was summoning up schoolboy French to ask for the gendarmerie when he saw its sign next to the post office, the entrance set back inside a cobbled court.

A dog slept on the stones, nose between its paws. As Seagram approached the open door, a gendarme emerged and stood with a cigarette cocked between two fingers. From cap to boots he was immaculate, the breeches seemingly out of a mould, the jacket good enough for Huntsman any day, the tie untouched by human hand. For so rural a place, he was ferociously dapper.

Seagram produced his Metropolitan Police identity card. 'I think you're expecting me. Chief Superintendent Seagram.'

Tapping away ash, the gendarme inspected the card with suitable care. He lifted his eyebrows and turned back into his office, inclining his head as though fair-minded enough not to exclude anything.

On his desk he pushed papers to and fro with a paper-knife. Finally he picked up a yellow sheet. 'Chief Superintendent Sea*gram*.' He stressed the second syllable as though already having to correct some minor deception. 'I have a notification.'

'Good.'

'You intend to call on Monsieur Venniker . . .'

'This afternoon.'

Behind the gendarme's head, a wasp was lethargically checking a closed window for an escape route. Seagram said, 'I expect you provided the information about him which reached us from Paris. My Commissioner was very grateful.' He had rehearsed it on the aircraft with the aid of his pocket dictionary, head turned away towards the window so that the woman in the seat next to him would not see his lips moving.

The other inclined his head again. But he was pleased too. 'I am at your disposal, Chief Superintendent, if I can be of any further assistance.'

'Are Venniker and the girl both at the château today?'

'He is there undoubtedly – he was buying bread in Mersac this morning. As for the girl, she has not been seen for some time. There is a rumour that she is in the south for medical treatment. He avoids answering questions about her. On the other hand he is now buying food for more than one person. The letters he was receiving from Nice have stopped. In my opinion . . .' the gendarme tossed his cigarette butt into the courtyard, a gesture of dialectic finality '. . . in my opinion she has now returned to the house.'

'There's still very little known about her, I suppose? Apart from the fact that she's British and was first seen about ten months ago.'

'Certainly she is without a history in France. She is believed to be a fabric designer.'

'Is there no one who visits the château and might have got to know her – postmen, garbage collectors?'

'The postman leaves letters in a box some way from the house. There is no . . .' the gendarme paused for a polite smile '. . . garbage collection.'

'But does Venniker work the land by himself?'

'An Italian helps with the lavender crop and in the orchards sometimes. But he never comes to Mersac, his home is on the other side of the valley.' The gendarme smiled again. To inquire that far afield, the smile said, would call for more than a piece or two of yellow paper from Paris.

Bougainvillea was arched about the window where the wasp

muttered. Seagram wiped his neck with a handkerchief. 'I understand Mr Venniker's reputation has been good since he came to live in your area.'

'He keeps to himself. Personally I find him very agreeable. He once helped me when my car had broken down. We have drunk a glass of wine together. He tries hard to work the land – it is not easy for him.' The gendarme flicked a minute quantity of ash from the breeches. 'He also likes to build.'

'To build?'

'With stone. When you visit him perhaps he will show you.'

Seagram shook his head in wonder. Venniker? A *stonemason*? 'If you wanted his help in an investigation, a very important one, would you have any doubts about approaching him?'

The other considered. 'No.' He looked through the open door at a child crying because it had dropped some eggs. 'But I should of course be able to explain to him the importance of co-operation. For him as a foreigner.'

I can see you doing it, Seagram thought; very well too.

'The investigation of which you have spoken . . .'

'. . . does not relate to matters here. Or anywhere else on French soil. You have my assurance.'

'Ah.' They exchanged smiles of impregnable courtesy.

Seagram took the Renault keys from his pocket. 'One more thing. Perhaps you'll show me the route to Château Larche.'

The wall map on which the gendarme traced it with the letter opener was dated 1938. 'The distance is about eight kilometres. Take the track to the left where the lavender fields begin. The original entrance drive to the château is further on but overgrown. I do not advise it for your car.'

From the doorway, he called after Seagram. 'Take care from the crossroads – the road is narrow. Will you be staying in Mersac tonight, Chief Superintendent?'

'Yes, at the hotel on the square. If you recommend it.'

'I shall speak personally to Madame.' It sounded as though it would make a difference.

Seagram switched on the Renault's ignition, watching the gendarme stroll back to his office. There was bougainvillea to scent the air if he chose to open the window at the back, a wasp to drowse the afternoon away with if he didn't. Would he like that? Once, full of metropolitan ambition, fascinated by big city crime, tempted by the feel of the leather armchairs in the Assistant Commissioner's office, he would have laughed. But what about now?

A few tourists were strolling about the square, looking for picture postcards. Old women gossiped. On the cobbles the dog still lay with his head between his paws. Soon perhaps the gendarme would get bored with the papers on his desk and emerge to smoke another cigarette. Suppose, thought Seagram, foot on the clutch, suppose someone let off a hundred-pound bomb in the middle of that? It could happen to you, *mon frère*, one day. Even in Mertac.

2

Beyond the crossroads, the route climbed to the edge of the *causse* on the other side of the valley. When he reached the plateau, Seagram was driving past silent, empty countryside once more. But this lacked the fertility of the approach to Mersac. It was parched and deserted, with dry-stone walls stumbling erratically into the distance; the fields enclosed by them were no longer cultivated. It was a land lacking life, devoid even of colour, except for a few mustard fields towards the western horizon.

Occasionally he passed the ruins of cottages. One was at a point that gave a glimpse of Mersac and the valley below. Seagram slowed to look. The inhabitants must once have done the same and asked themselves why they should break their backs on the limestone of the *causse* when, down there, men could sit at their doors in the evening, watching the peaches grow.

The lavender crop was easy to find, its scent greeting Seagram at a dip in the road. Following the track through the fields, he reached an orchard of stunted apple trees and beyond that a stone barn. In the near wall of the barn the windows had rotted frames; but the roof showed signs of recent repair. An aged Citroen 2CV stood in the barn's shade, with a hen dozing on its bonnet, looking more than ever like a joke car.

The track divided, a minor fork disappearing away to Seagram's left. He drove on; then, round a bend with a masking line of oak trees came in sight of what was clearly the gatehouse to the château. A little run-down, he thought; but why expect more of a gatehouse, or indeed of Venniker? The clock face above the arch of the gatehouse had been bleached by the sun. Pale golden fingers picked out a time no more than twenty minutes different from Seagram's Omega.

Parking the Renault under one of the oaks, Seagram walked

to the gatehouse arch. Here at last would be the vista of Venniker's pile, decayed and impoverished no doubt, but a château
after all. He gazed. There were perhaps fifty metres of stone-
slabbed track, with turf and ornamental bushes to either side.
At the end of that – nothing. Nothing at all, except for hillocks
of tumbled stone buried in grass. Like the cottages on the
causse, the château had gone a long time ago.

Along a minor path of gravel which took a more direct route
to the barn than the track along which he had driven, came the
crunch of footsteps. The hair was paler, bleached by the sun;
otherwise it seemed that five years had made no change to Venniker's appearance. The walk might be slower, a shade more
relaxed. But it hadn't lost its air of slightly languorous vigilance.

'Looking for Shepherd Market,' Seagram said. He stretched
out his hand. 'Can you help me?'

He watched Venniker reach back into memory, not quite
getting there. Then his chin lifted as though a breeze had touched
him. 'Seagram.' He gave no sign of real surprise. But that had
never been his way. 'You've shaved off your moustache.'

'The razor slipped one morning.'

'I see.' He took Seagram's hand, shook it warily.

In front of the gatehouse a table stood beneath a chestnut
tree with a couple of benches beside it. Venniker put down the
bowl of eggs he had been carrying. The sun had broken through
at last; the heat promised to become suffocating. Seagram wiped
sweat from his forehead. 'I like your address.'

'Rather misleading, I'm afraid.'

'Does it matter?'

'Unfortunately, there *are* disadvantages. The château's marked
with the wrong symbol on the tourist maps. People looking for
culture arrive and ask to be shown round. When I tell them
there's only a heap of stones they tend to blame me.'

'It must have been impressive once.'

'Yes. Although you can't see from here it was built on the
edge of what's almost a cliff.'

'When did it disappear?'

'During the Revolution. It was burned down with the family
inside it. Most of the masonry from the house was carted away
and used elsewhere. The smaller buildings weren't touched but

some of them just crumbled – nobody lived here for years. I tinker with what's left.'

Venniker smiled briefly, that smile that was half-bitter, half-watchful.

'How's London?'

'Still there. Too many people.'

'Bombs as well.'

'Bombs as well.'

Venniker picked a straw from amongst the eggs. 'Things are quieter in the Lot, you'll find.' He gestured to the benches and they sat down. The sky was almost completely blue now. The only sound came from the birds in the chestnut tree. Seagram thought: suppose I ducked out to a place like this, followed in Venniker's footsteps. He wrote a news story in his mind: Away from it All in the Lot – Senior Scotland Yard Man resigns to grow lavender. Says I have no regrets, I am glad to leave to others job of coppering for idle, foolish, never-learn-their-lesson British public. And a soldier's farewell to the great British Press too.

'Well ...' Venniker's eyes were on the middle distance. 'You were just passing, were you, and decided to drop in?'

'Would you have believed that?'

'I don't think so.'

From the direction of the barn came a sudden cry, repeated twice, a desolate despairing sound. 'What the hell ...' said Seagram.

'A peacock.'

'You keep a *peacock*?'

'Six in fact. Rather too many. Delusions of grandeur can come quite cheap here.' Something brightly coloured was visible, moving near the 2CV. 'Why not take a couple home with you?'

'Peacocks might not settle down too well in Lewisham.'

'You live in Lewisham?'

'Yes.'

Venniker shook his head. 'Somehow I never thought of you living anywhere. A camp bed in an office at the Yard perhaps, but not a house.'

'It's there all right. I just don't see much of it.'

14

'It must have cost you a lot of trouble to locate me. I've never told anyone in England this address.'

'As a matter of fact we asked the French police to locate you. I need your help.'

'You – or the Yard?'

'Is that an important distinction?'

'It might be.'

It was said lightly enough, but warningly. There was a ditch there that might take some crossing. Venniker rose to his feet. 'You must be thirsty, I know I am. I'll get a bottle of wine. Hang on.'

He went off to the gatehouse, carrying the bowl of eggs. He was still an attractive figure, looking healthier than he did during his London days. Yet, even here, there was that air about him Seagram remembered from their first meeting in Shepherd Market, the night Brinkham had shot himself and Seagram had gone to pull in Venniker because it looked like murder; that air of an outsider. The drinking club in the Market that Venniker had run had seemed in some ways the obvious place for him. There if anywhere he ought to have looked at home. But whatever environment he moved in, he would always be alien. Once, he must have had recognizable roots. But Seagram had never uncovered them. By the time they met, they were too subterranean, only hinted at now and then by some ironical recollection or a vowel too flat for a southern English upbringing.

The sun had swung round far enough to reach inside the gatehouse arch. A vine grew across the arch and the whole of the front of the building. On the stone behind its leaves Seagram could see a blue tinge where Venniker had been using a foliar spray. All the windows were wide open but there was no sign of life in them. If the girl really was there, she was keeping out of sight.

The wine came in a bottle with no label. 'Your own?' he asked, ready to believe anything of this new life style.

'The supermarket in Cahors. Sorry.' Venniker handed him a glass and pointed towards the barn. The peacocks were advancing in arrowhead formation. 'They've decided that they'll come and entertain you.'

Seagram stretched city shoes before him and drank. Lewisham

15

and the Yard seemed a long way off. He felt a great reluctance to face the effort of persuasion that lay ahead.

Venniker had lit a cigarette. 'What's brought you?'

'We have a problem you're in a position to help us with.'

'Me?' He laughed. 'I don't even know anybody in the rackets now.'

'Somebody we're interested in is a man you once knew quite well. His name is Jewkes.'

'Jewkes ...' Venniker was reaching back again, but it was harder and further this time.

'Moley Jewkes. You shared a cell at Bedgley Prison for twelve months.'

Venniker said, 'Ah, Moley.' He looked away along the line of oaks. 'Moley Jewkes. He used to have dreams about eating caramel toffees. I never see them in a shop without remembering Moley's dreams.'

'Moley's dreams are more sophisticated now.'

'When I left Bedgley he still had some time to do. I can't remember what he was in for.'

'Fraud – bucket shops – nothing very ambitious. He went back to it after he was released. Then he disappeared. A few months ago he showed up again – but in Brussels this time. Plenty of gravy now. He has an import-export racket, a sleek car and an even sleeker mistress who's said to be half-Indonesian. One side of his business is bamboo furniture. The other side is drugs – heroin mainly.'

The peacocks had decided that nothing interesting was going to happen and were moving off towards the door of the gatehouse.

'What am I expected to do about it?' Venniker asked.

'Contact Jewkes in Brussels and win his confidence. Enough to enable us to find out who the big boys behind him are.'

'He's not big himself?'

'No, he only fetches and carries.' Seagram traced the grain of the table top with his fingers. 'I can't promise the earth. But if you'll do it I'll make it well worth your while.'

'It would be impossible for me to be away from this place for a long stretch.'

'With luck this will only take a few days. If it dragged on you could slip back for visits provided you weren't cutting your cover story to pieces.' He lifted his eyes. 'Isn't there anyone to keep an eye on things?'

'An Italian who lives across the valley helps me. But not every day. I'd have to pay him to come over more.'

'We'd add that to your expenses.'

Venniker's gaze was on the gatehouse. His eyes were shadowed underneath. For the first time it occurred to Seagram that although he looked well enough he was under some strain. 'I quite liked Moley,' said Venniker. He was temporizing, as much with himself as with Seagram.

'You wouldn't like what he's into.'

'Heroin.'

'That's only part of the story. The less interesting part.' Seagram drank more of the wine, trying to decide how far to go. 'Look, you don't have to decide this minute. There's a lot more to tell. Have a meal with me tonight. I'm staying at the hotel in Mersac – the one on the square.'

Venniker sat silent. It was almost as though he had stopped listening.

'With a holding like this I don't suppose it's easy making ends meet.'

'You checked that out with the locals, of course . . .'

'Does it matter?' He watched Venniker as he brooded.

'In any case . . .' Seagram began again but Venniker had turned away, his face tightening. Music was coming from the gatehouse, an orchestra; it was playing something that sounded medieval. In the ordinary way indifferent to sounds except for the evidence they offered of other facts, Seagram found himself listening, vaguely moved.

'What's that?'

'A record player.'

'I mean the piece.'

'It's something by Vivaldi.'

He knew the name, that was all. He drank and listened again.

Perhaps the whole of his life would have had a different flavour if, quite near its beginning, he had sat under a chestnut tree with a bottle of wine and peacocks for company on a summer's afternoon while music like this played. 'A change from Shepherd Market,' he said.

'That's why I came here.'

'And you never regret it?'

'Never, I don't want the past back.' Venniker was looking at him. 'None of it.' His eyes were cold.

It was a bad moment. Then Venniker put his hand on Seagram's arm. 'I didn't mean that personally.' He gave a brief smile. 'But that's the way I feel.'

The music was becoming louder. Somebody had turned up the volume of the record player to its maximum. The sound poured in a flood from the door and windows of the gatehouse. It seemed to have become a sort of proclamation, faintly sinister.

The side of Venniker's jaw was white. As he started to rise to his feet, Seagram pre-empted him; there was probably nothing more to be gained now and perhaps something to be lost. 'I think I'll get back to Mersac and have a bath.' He stood, mopping his neck. 'Do they actually *run* to a bath in that hotel?'

'A primrose one sat on the terrace all this spring – they must have fitted it by now.' Venniker was making a great effort to pretend to ignore the noise. 'Ask for Eloise to scrub you down. She's the daughter of the house. About two hundred and ten pounds.'

'That's what she charges?'

'That's what she weighs.'

With his hand on the door of the Renault, Seagram said, 'So, you'll come tonight...'

'Perhaps.'

'About eight thirty then...'

'I'll see.' Venniker wanted him to be gone, it was obvious. But as Seagram started the engine he said, 'It matters to you *personally* – this case?'

'Very much.'

'You're in charge of the investigation?'

'As much of it as would involve you. You'd have to deal with nobody else.'

He nodded. 'Well ...' Stepping back, he raised a hand. 'Until tonight.'

Driving past the barn Seagram noticed that the peacocks were back in the shadows. They all seemed to be ignoring his car except one. It gave him that raucous lonely cry. The noise of the music followed him for longer as he drove along the track through the apple orchard and the lavender fields. It was, in its way, another sort of cry.

3

The bedroom door was open. Opal lay on the bed with her head turned towards the window. One hand plucked at the mattress buttons through the sheet, the other hovered above the knobs of the record player on the floor. The noise seemed to shake even the walls.

Venniker leaned across the bed and switched the volume down. Her eyes turned towards him and she smiled. She appeared perfectly relaxed, immune to the din.

'Aren't you deafened yet?'

'No.'

'Your ear drums are tougher than mine.'

She stretched hands and feet to the corners of the bed, yawning. 'When the sun came out I watched it lift across the valley. It was like a running tide. I thought the Vivaldi would go with it.'

'It went all right,' he said. He sat down on the bed. On the floor by his feet were her shirt and jeans. 'Did you sleep?'

'Yes. When I woke up I felt marvellous. For the first time I felt . . . free.'

Venniker gazed more closely into her face. She had altogether lost that aura of listless indifference. The skin still looked drawn and a little greasy; yet not as much as even the day before. Perhaps they really were over the hump. But he wouldn't be betting on it yet.

'You don't believe me, do you?'

'I believe you. Just let it happen. You don't have to force it.'

'How do you know that isn't exactly what someone like me has to do – force it? Or be forced?'

He picked the clothes up from the floor and put them on a chair. 'I doubt it.'

'Why don't you tell me that if I haven't kicked it this time you won't pick up the pieces. That I can go back to Rome and rot. Why don't you say that?'

She was half-serious. Underneath he knew she was still frightened.

'Perhaps I will.'

'Not you.'

He shrugged.

Opal touched his cheek with her fingers. They were cool, a little damp. She moved them to his neck and lifted her head to place her lips against his. Her mouth began soft then became a hard ring of tissue. She stroked him with her other hand.

As at every other similar moment since her return from the clinic, the sensation of her touch produced in him first tension and then a growing melancholy. At first he had found reasons, excuses: the sourness of her breath, the thinness that made her seem so fragile, the desperation of her attempts to create sensation in him. Gradually he had faced up to the fact that it was not so simple. Something had happened to him. He was neutered, it seemed, and without a hint of warning. He was like a man who had been spread-eagled on some shadowless reach of the limestone *causse* until the sun had burned the quick out of him.

When she turned her head away, he said, 'Sorry.'

She wouldn't speak. He stroked her hair. There was a lozenge of sunlight across her shoulder and he kissed it. She shrugged his head away and reached to the bedside table for a cigarette. 'It's me, isn't it? You can't stand me.'

'No.'

'Yes, it's me.'

Impasse, he thought. In one way he was glad to have got there so quickly.

They lay in silence, watching the sky through the window that looked over the valley. She placed her cigarette between his lips. He pulled on it and replaced it in her mouth. She smiled at him. 'Don't worry,' she said. 'You don't have to force it.'

He could just hear the labouring of a truck as it climbed up the road on to the *causse*. For the sound to reach over this distance meant it was one of the giant freighters. It was the only noise that ever came from the world passing by outside. 'Who was that who came earlier?' Opal asked.

'A man I used to know in London.'

'Clever to find you – I thought nobody had your address.'

'He's that sort of man.'

'Trouble?'

'No, not trouble. There might even be money in it.'

He realized he hadn't decided how much he should tell her about Seagram. But he was spared making up his mind for the moment because some other thought had struck her. 'I forgot to tell you. While you were out this morning they telephoned from Montauban about the lavender crop. No deal apparently. They said their requirement for the year isn't as large as they expected. But they thought there'd be bound to be another company that would be interested. There must be plenty we could try.'

'I doubt it.'

'Why?'

'Because there's going to be a glut. Aldo says so.'

'Why be so pessimistic before you've tried?'

'I'm facing facts. There wouldn't be such a good crop if there weren't going to be a glut. It's a law of bloody nature.'

She hesitated, chewing her lip. 'About the clinic bill . . .'

'Don't worry, it's going to be settled. I've allowed for it. That's not affected by what we do or don't get for the lavender.'

'I'll pay you back when I get a job.'

He stared. 'What job?'

'I've decided to go to London for a while.'

'When did you decide that?'

'When I woke up this afternoon. I knew I was going to be all right. I want to make some money and pay you back.'

He turned her face towards him with his hand. 'You don't owe me anything and you don't pay me anything. So you don't need to go.'

'You want me to stay?'

Cautiously he said, 'Until you've got better reasons of your own for wanting to go.'

She gave him a twisted smile. 'Anyway,' he said, 'leave it for a while, there's no hurry is there?'

The afternoon faded. Insects flew in and out of the bedroom, waiting for the lamps. Perhaps she really had kicked it, he thought. No more hiding places, no more denials, no more scenes, no more treatment. No more bills. It was conceivable. He had never allowed himself to consider quite dispassionately whether she really had the will-power to come through. In these past few months he had been too busy trying to convince *her* that she had it. Well, if she truly believed she had beaten it, ought he to stop her going?

Venniker sat up abruptly. 'Our visitor this afternoon was a Chief Superintendent from Scotland Yard called Seagram. He was the one in charge of the investigation into the death of Arthur Brinkham.'

'The Cabinet Minister who used to visit your club – the man who shot himself . . . ?'

'Yes. I owe Seagram a good deal. If it weren't for him I probably wouldn't be here now.'

'Why do you owe him anything? All he did was prove that Brinkham hadn't been murdered but had actually committed suicide. That your being with him beforehand had nothing to do with it. That was his job – finding out the facts.'

He knew she hadn't really understood when he had first told the story to her, the time he had woken from a nightmare soon after he had brought her back to Larche. She could talk trendily about the fuzz, affect that weary cynicism of her generation. But when it came to grasping the reality of what could happen with a really bent policeman on the other side of the table, she couldn't begin.

'It was also the job of the copper in Bedgley who got me sent down earlier by planting the evidence to build his case. But he didn't see it that way. All he wanted was to cover up the fact that he'd made a mistake in saying I was involved and after that to get a nice spread in the local newspaper. That's how things were done in Bedgley.

'Seagram wasn't any less ambitious. He liked getting convictions too. And what he was faced with was a dead politician, a gun that had my fingerprints on it as well as the politician's and proof that I'd been in the house at about the right time. And who was I? A man who'd been convicted and sent to prison once in Bedgley. A man who had a grievance against Brinkham. Seagram could have charged me with murder the same night and nobody would have thought he was wrong. But he listened to what I had to say and believed it. Then he made it his business to prove I didn't kill Brinkham. Do you still think I don't owe him anything?'

Opal sighed. 'No, I see what you mean. But why was he here?'

'He's asked for my help.'

'He wants you to go to London?'

'No, Brussels. The people he's investigating operate from there. I knew one of them once, shared a cell with him at Bedgley prison. Seagram wants me to get alongside him.' He pulled off his shirt. 'I've said I'll have a meal with him in Mersac tonight and talk it over.'

She traced his spine with a finger. 'How long would you have to be away?'

'Not more than a few days. At a time, that is.' He turned his head. 'I could ask Aldo to come more often. Would you be all right?'

'Of course I would. It's not dangerous?'

He laughed. The possibility hadn't struck him. He thought of Moley Jewkes dreaming of caramel toffees. 'I shouldn't think so.'

'When you come back I'm still going to earn the money to pay for the clinic.'

Venniker stood up and went to the window. 'I told you to forget about it. Anyway, why the rush?'

'Because I've got to try. Somewhere you're not around to help. I've got to try.'

He had no answer. For the first time he thought of the silence with her not there.

4

The terrace of the Hotel du Midi overlooked Mersac's only square. Amongst the geranium tubs along the edge of the terrace, Seagram sat in his shirt sleeves and watched the *boules* players below. The game was conducted under a street lamp, the players moving slowly through light to shadow and back again.

Beyond was a café with tables on the pavement. Those drinking at the tables occasionally called advice to the players. Boys sat astride motor cycles and chatted up girls. It was the small-talking end to a hot summer's day, with the cats suddenly alert in doorways and the air smelling of woodsmoke.

In London, if there was smoke tonight, it would not be from wood. Moving through it, slowly and gingerly, would be the Bomb Squad boys, scooping up the fragments for Forensic's little games.

The 2CV Seagram had seen in the shade of Venniker's barn appeared from a corner of the square, drove past the café and parked. A moment later he saw Venniker on the fringe of the *boules* players wearing a light jacket. One of the players called to him and he pointed in the direction of the hotel; waving a finger in mock admonition, the player turned back to the game.

'Did they want you to join them?' he asked, as Venniker sat down beside him on the terrace.

'Not quite. In about fifty years time perhaps.'

'You don't sound particularly at home yet.'

'I don't feel particularly out of place either.'

'No nostalgia for England?'

'Only when I'm very drunk. Did you get your bath?'

'Eloise unlocked the door personally. She also issued me with a very small tablet of soap. But she didn't offer to scrub me down.'

'Perhaps she's discovered you're a policeman.'

'Perhaps.' He wondered vaguely what the gendarme *had* said about him to Madame. 'You don't think it would go in my favour?'

'I expect Eloise prefers the law to keep its distance. Like most people. But you must have learned to live with that by now.'

Seagram reached for his drink. 'Sometimes I forget and imagine I'm a human being.'

They had the meal served on the terrace. Two other tables were occupied besides theirs, one by a family of German tourists, the other by an aged couple who arrived with their own bottle of mineral water. After Madame had taken orders, Eloise appeared to serve the food. She exchanged greetings in French with Venniker, her manner perceptibly warmer than at the bathroom door.

'Tell me your secret,' said Seagram, as she moved away again.

'She's convinced I'm an English gentleman. I rely on you not to tell her the truth.'

'That could be part of our deal.'

Venniker rubbed his eyes; they still looked tired. 'How did you find out Moley was into the drugs racket?'

'It was the Burmese police who first put us on to it. In Rangoon last year they were keeping surveillance on a man who used to be one of the chief lieutenants of Lo-Hsing Han. Do you know who I'm talking about?'

'No.'

'Lo-Hsing Han was *the* opium king in Burma in the sixties. The lieutenant was named Chei Win. He was said to control a factory on the Thai border where the opium was processed into heroin. The heroin was of very high quality – nothing like the Chinese stuff they normally push on Gerrard Street – up-market stuff. The Burmese surveillance team saw Chei Win make contact with a foreigner whom they followed back to a hotel. He'd come in from Brussels a few days before and was English, according to his papers. They sent the details to the Yard with a photostat of his passport. We replied the next day with the result of a CRO check and said no doubt they'd give the Englishman a going-over when he left the country. Answer – deafening silence.

'Presumably something political happened in the interval – we never knew what. When we finally got a reply out of them it was to the effect that everything before had been a great mistake. The informants had turned out to be fabricators, the factory on the Thai border was really producing tobacco and so on ...

'This was annoying because the name on the passport – which was quite a good forgery – had been an alias used once by Moley Jewkes. I don't know whether you ever knew it – Rex Arundel.'

Venniker shook his head. 'No. But Moley always aspired. He would have been proud of that.' He smiled at Eloise approaching with a tray; there was a warmth to his charm that Seagram had forgotten. 'Does he run the stuff into England as well?'

Seagram watched Eloise spooning an artichoke like a young cabbage alongside his roast duck. 'Somebody else does that. We haven't been able to identify the channels. The pushing operation is very secure, very professional and rather unusual. The first sign we had was an increase in heroin use in the more expensive public schools and two of the universities. Then we noticed Service units being affected. Most of the users had been introduced to heroin in the same way. They'd first been given cocaine to sniff. The coke came in small plastic containers with a picture of a moon daisy on the side. They were known as 'daisies' and it became very smart in schools if you could produce one. They were cult objects in no time at all. Now what always stopped cocaine taking off on the British drugs scene before has been the high basic cost. But the pushers handing out the daisies were apparently treating them as though coke costs no more than hash. Which is economic nonsense.

'It took our drugs people at the Yard a while before they could swallow the true explanation. The daisies were a come-on, a loss-leader by which the pusher established a relationship with a new customer, got him persuaded that drugs didn't seem too dangerous after all and prepared him for a switch from coke-sniffing, which is non-addictive of course, to heroin injection which would hook him effectively. But even the heroin is being sold at prices which are causing gloom amongst the other people in the business.'

'Why should the pushers sell below the price the stuff normally fetches? Once they've got their supplies it's presumably an independent operation for them.'

'No, it isn't. There seems to be some quite sophisticated control over the pushers. We haven't fathomed how it works but if they're found charging more than the rate prescribed by the suppliers they lose their supply. One of them was shot dead outside his house the other day because of a ploy to increase his take beyond what had been laid down.'

'If you know that much you ought to be able to get inside the organization through one of the pushers.'

'It doesn't work – we've tried it. In fact we already have a pusher playing with us. The organization on the supply side is too tight. Supply and payment is on the old Russian *dubok* system – the pusher places his cash in an agreed hiding place which is invariably somewhere that makes effective surveillance impossible and he collects his fresh supplies from a different hiding place the next day. He gets instructions about the hiding places by post. If he wants emergency contact he has to put a pre-arranged code message in the *Daily Telegraph* and wait for a telephone call. But he won't *see* anyone.'

Venniker shook his head. 'You mean there's never any personal contact?'

'Not after the initial business deal. As a security operation it's the best I've ever struck – more like an espionage ring than a drug-peddling job. And it's paying off in more ways than one. For sixty years the back room boys in the Home Office have been telling the world that the drugs problem in Britain is under control. In some places I doubt if that's any longer true.'

The old man who had brought his mineral water with him to the next table had taken off his jacket. In the terrace lamplight, the metal adjustment clips on his braces twinkled as he bent forward to scour his plate with bread. 'So it's the supply end of this racket you want to get at – the people who are producing the stuff and pumping it into England,' Venniker said.

'Yes. But ...' Seagram broke off, while Eloise removed their empty bottle.

'... But what?'

'There's something more serious tied up with the drugs racket. I wouldn't be here if it were just that. Let's have more wine.' Honeysuckle mingled with kitchen scents in Seagram's nostrils. Suddenly he was aware that time was slowing down to an agreeable crawl. He had begun to relax and he didn't want this dinner on a lamplit terrace to be just another part of the job. He sat back in his chair. 'What made you choose this particular place to settle in?'

'Accident. I knew nothing about the Lot before I came here – had no idea where it was on the map even. This happened to be where I stopped driving.'

'I remember what you said the night Brinkham shot himself – when I still wasn't sure I wouldn't be charging you with murder. You said you'd just made up your mind to leave London. I'm going south, you said, a long way south.'

Venniker watched Eloise uncorking the new bottle.

'When you'd closed your investigation I realized I hadn't any reason for not doing what I'd said. I sold the club, paid back the money I owed on it and took off. I told nobody. My father had just died and there wasn't anyone left who needed to know. Vaguely I thought I was going to settle in Provence – run a bar on the coast perhaps. But when I got there it seemed to be full of the people I was trying to get away from – hairdressers who'd made it in Mayfair, interior decorators who'd made it in Manchester, farmers who'd sold out to property developers, developers who'd sold out to investment companies, all the old gang. They weren't even crooks – just people who'd been stripping a carcase and wanted their place in the sun while they digested it. So I came back inland. The car broke down a few kilometres out of Mersac. The sun was shining. Apart from the tourists at the camping site everybody looked as though he'd lived here for ages. So I stayed. I bought the gatehouse and everything with it from a man who swore the orchards and the lavender crop would keep me. He was lying, of course – I found out later that the place had been for sale more than five years.'

'But you've survived ...'

'I've found out how little one needs.' Venniker flicked a crumb from the tablecloth, smiling. 'Barring disasters.'

In the pâtisserie next to the café, a woman was wiping glass shelves while a child played beside her. 'You still haven't told me the rest of the story,' he said.

Seagram stirred himself and sighed. 'Briefly it's this. The U.S. Drugs Enforcement Administration has a small team in Brussels. That team runs an agent who has met Jewkes and as a result acquired some vague information about the organization he's tied up with. At first he thought it was a straightforward drugs operation targeted against the U.K. and, apparently, nowhere else. Then he stumbled across something that put a new complexion on the business. The drugs are subsidiary to the main purpose of the organization. In return for getting the stuff at a very keen price and with absolute security, the professionals who distribute it have had to provide something rather unusual. Explosions.'

'*Explosions?*'

'You must have read in the French press the details of this new wave of bombings – big country houses, the offices of large industrial companies, Balmoral – nobody killed but plenty of publicity.'

'What's the motive?'

'Political presumably. But it's not a political group we know the slightest thing about. We need to get more facts very urgently. They've taken good care not to kill anyone yet but how long is that going to last? The Americans are not hopeful their source is going to pick up any more and in any case they're very coy about him – we haven't been able to put any questions or see him ourselves.' Seagram paused and waited for Venniker to look up. 'You can understand now why I want your help. We *must* get inside.'

'Are addicts being used to plant the bombs – is that what you're saying?'

'It's possible but I don't think it's likely. Those bombs – the early ones anyway – were planted, if my guess is correct, by professional criminals working on contract to the drugs distributors. It's not hard to arrange that sort of thing particularly if nobody has to be killed.'

Venniker shook his head. 'It doesn't hang together.'

'What doesn't?'

'Blowing things up ... and drug-pushing.'

'You may not think so. But it's happening.'

Behind Venniker a searchlight beam suddenly split the sky. It was being directed from a position Seagram judged was near the Agricultural Cooperative's building. By degrees the beam's angle became smaller. Out of the night with dramatic sharpness, the *donjon* materialized.

Venniker turned to follow Seagram's gaze. 'Bastille Day soon – they're getting ready. Mersac provides the *lumière*, the *son* just arrives of its own accord.' He drained his glass. 'So the secret to all this is in Brussels ...'

'It must be. The main artery for the drugs runs through the place. Orders are given there. Jewkes lives there.'

At the German tourists' table there was a small commotion. They were being made to wait a very long time for something. Eloise was in attendance. Her massive shoulders lifted enigmatically; then she turned her back on the Germans. Venniker said, 'If you go south from here across the *causse* for a few kilometres you come to Veyrelau. In May 1944 twelve people in that village were shut up in the bakery. Petrol was poured over it and it was then burned down. Nobody got out. A German SS unit did it as a reprisal for some assistance given to the Maquis. Amongst the people in the bakery were an uncle and two cousins of Eloise.'

Seagram watched the old man at the other table near them take a clasp-knife from his pocket to deal with the fruit. Carefully he sliced an apple against his palm and handed the pieces to his wife before selecting one for himself. 'It's difficult to imagine in this countryside.'

'Two weeks later people got up one morning and looked at the *donjon*. It had a flagpole in those days. Nailed to the flagpole was the dead body of a German officer in full uniform. A red flag was flying on the pole above. There were more reprisals – in this square down there. Fifty men and women were shot. A German needs to be aware of things like that before he takes a holiday here. Because 1944 was only last week in Quercy.'

'How long ago was the Hundred Years War in Quercy?'

Venniker was grinning. 'Long enough. Just.' He sat back; he looked relaxed himself now. 'Why are you involved in this investigation, Seagram? Drugs and bombs are both dealt with by specialists back at the Yard, aren't they? Your side was straight crime.'

'The Bomb Squad have been given some extra support from C.I.D. because the politicians are getting very jumpy. But the important factor was – I knew you. And we got along.'

When Venniker made no reply, he said, 'We *did* get along, didn't we?' But Venniker was staring over his shoulder. Seagram turned.

A girl stood in the open doorway between the terrace and the hotel dining-room. She wore a long-sleeved cotton dress that brushed the ground. Her hair was slightly disordered as though she had been walking in a breeze. Against the lighted room behind her, she had an insubstantial, almost ghostly quality. She smiled at Venniker. 'Surprised?' she said.

5

Venniker got up from the table slowly. He was doing his best not to look surprised. Walking over to them the girl took the chair facing Seagram. She lifted a hand in greeting to him. 'Hullo.'

She was beautiful, even though she was paper-thin – pale blonde hair, soft as a child's, the eyes like dark smudges in a dead white face, the mouth very wide. Venniker said, 'Opal, this is Superintendent Seagram – sorry, *Chief* Superintendent Seagram.' He pronounced the word with mock solemnity, as though he had recovered his composure but Seagram was sure he hadn't. 'From Scotland Yard.'

Seagram reached for a glass from the serving board behind him and placed it beside her. 'Are you living here – or just staying?'

'Both.' She smiled, then looked triumphantly at Venniker. 'Aren't you wondering how I got to Mersac tonight?'

'Yes.'

'On the Honda.'

He was pouring her some wine. 'In that dress?'

'I tied it round my waist. Rather draughty.'

The square neck of the dress was crocheted. It had the sort of simplicity that cost a good deal of money although it looked as though it had known better days. Opal said, 'Actually, I wasn't sure when I started I was really going to arrive. But it seemed a pity to give up once I got to the end of the track. The woman who sits outside the cottage by the bridge thought she was seeing a ghost.'

'Where did you first meet Paul,' Seagram asked.

'In Rome.'

Venniker cut in rather fast. 'I made a visit there about a year ago – trying to collect from somebody who owed me money.

33

Opal was at a loose end. When she heard I was on my own at Larche she took pity.'

Seagram smiled politely at her. 'I envy him.'

'Our wonderful fuzz,' she said. 'Are you all like this back home now?'

He winced inwardly but she wasn't sneering, she seemed genuinely warm.

'Actually,' she went on, 'it wasn't that way at all. Paul always writes himself down. The man I'd been living with in Rome had just died. I had no money suddenly. I had other problems too. Paul took me in hand. I owe him ... a great deal.'

Eloise brought coffee. Seagram said to Opal, 'So here you are.'

'For a while. Coming straight from London you must find it pretty quiet.'

Seagram thought of the music shouting out of the windows of the gatehouse as he sat under the chestnut tree. He wanted to say – what exactly can't *you* stand about the quiet?

Opal had placed her hands on the table, gripping the base of the wine glass between them. Seagram stared at her wrists. They were very slender, very flat; like – what? Something a long time ago ... the sheep's bones he had used as clappers when he was a boy in Somerset. Lifting his eyes to her face again he realized it was not just thin. She was either ill or had been recently. So the gendarme's story of medical treatment had probably been right.

Venniker said, 'I might be making a trip to Brussels. You could come too, if you like.' He avoided Seagram's eyes.

Seagram began, 'I don't ...' but Opal was already saving the day for him.

'If you don't mind I think I'd rather stay here.' She looked at Seagram. 'Is he going there for you? What will he have to do?'

'Make contact with someone he used to know. Meet the people he works for. That's all.'

'Not risky?'

'We'll be very careful.'

'Am I going to be told any more?'

'It's best if we leave it at that. For you and everybody.

There'll be a story for his trip which you can use with anybody who asks. You'll find it easier if you're not involved. I'd be grateful if you'd forget my visit and who I am.'

Her expression was at first amused; then she shrugged. 'All right ...' On balance she meant it, he judged. But would she feel the same tomorrow, next week? 'Are many people likely to inquire?' he asked.

'I don't see people,' she said, 'so you don't have to worry.'

She shivered suddenly. 'It's not so warm.' Seagram watched one of her hands reach out across the table until Venniker covered it with his own. Behind them the searchlight which had been at rest for a while swung sharply up at the sky before settling again on the *donjon*. The blocks of stone from which it was built looked enormous even at this distance. 'It's very formidable that tower,' he said.

Venniker shook his head. 'In fact it's falling down. They've stopped visitors going inside this summer. The locals won't spend money on repairs because they say it's the responsibility of the Ministry of Beaux Arts. I told the mayor he could have my labour for a small sum – or even for nothing at all if others would help. He was just amused.'

'You like building things?'

'It began as necessity – I had to fix the barn. I found I enjoyed doing it – I don't know why. Just off the main track to the gatehouse there's something you won't have noticed – a pigeon-house. You were a nobody in Quercy in the old days if you hadn't got a *pigeonnier*. I'm repairing it. I've done the stonework but there's some tiling to finish. Of course it isn't the slightest use.' He grinned; the look of wary vigilance had disappeared.

'You could always keep pigeons in it.'

Opal said, 'Building is his vice. He's abandoned all the others.' She was smiling at Venniker as she said it; but the atmosphere was charged with something Seagram couldn't gauge. She shivered once more and almost closed her eyes. Venniker said, 'Do you want to go inside?'

'It seemed stifling when I started out.'

He stood up. 'We ought to be going anyway.' He was tense again, still holding her hand.

'Is it settled then?' Seagram said. 'About Brussels?'

'I'd like to think a bit more. I'll telephone you here in the morning.'

Ah, he thought, the old Venniker: don't tie me down, don't assume I'm committed, I may have another option. He made himself smile. Opal stretched out the hand Venniker was not holding to touch Seagram; her fingers pressed the inside of his forearm. 'I'll persuade him.' It was almost a gesture of alliance.

She turned to Venniker. 'What about the Honda?'

'We'll leave it in the yard – I'll pick it up some time.'

At the door of the hotel, while Venniker was moving the Honda round to the back, Seagram said, 'I missed your name. Opal . . .'

'Rayner, Opal Rayner.'

'From . . .?'

'Rome.' She wasn't going to volunteer any more. 'Will you come again?'

'I hope so. Perhaps when we've finished in Brussels.'

She gazed into the night. 'I may not be here. But knowing me I probably shall.' He held out his hand. Taking it she moved lightly against him. He breathed the perfume from her neck for a moment. The movement seemed to offer no invitation, was scarcely even an act of flirtation. But he knew that an instinct he had felt when glimpsing her for the first time on the hotel terrace had not been wrong.

The street lamp by which the game of *boules* had been played was no longer lit. As Opal and Venniker moved away from Seagram into the shadows where the 2CV was parked, the long dress seemed to have a luminous quality. Once, Seagram knew, he would have reacted to the girl as to a danger signal; danger to ambition, to judgement, to peace of mind. Now he could view her simply as a threat to the security of the operation in Brussels. Sexual vanity and its fantasies had ceased to be a scourge. Vulnerability was something that others suffered from; or so he believed. Later, catching his eye in the mirror over the basin in his bedroom as he brushed his teeth, recalling again the scent of the skin and her body receding into the night, he felt the smallest tremor of doubt. But after he had turned out the light, he slept dreamlessly without another thought of her.

He was seated awkwardly by his bedside table the next morning, trying to contain the demolition of his croissant on the saucer of his coffee cup when he was called to the telephone by Eloise.

It was Venniker. 'Sorry if I got you out of bed.'

'You didn't – I've already been for a walk.'

He wiped a scrap of butter from the corner of his mouth with the paper napkin he had carried with him from the bedroom. 'But while I think of it, what is the bloody logic of not giving one a plate at breakfast in this country?'

'Less washing-up.'

'Ah,' he said.

'Your proposition . . .'

'Yes.'

'We didn't discuss how much it would be worth. In money.'

'No, we didn't.'

'If I said I needed 3000 francs pretty soon . . .'

'That's all right.'

'Win or lose?'

'If you do your best you'll get it whether you're successful or not. And if you pull it off there'll be a bonus. Come down later this morning and we'll settle all the details.'

Seagram listened to silence at the other end. After a while Venniker said quietly, 'Right.'

Strolling again through Mersac afterwards, Seagram completed his inspection of churches, shops, the *mairie* and finally the *donjon*. A faded signboard on the tower announced it was XIIth century. A rose he couldn't put a name to climbed up one side. Even as close as this, there was no sign of the decay Venniker had mentioned. But the door was padlocked and another sign nailed upon it warned against approach. Stepping back he let his gaze run up to the top of the tower. Once, on a morning perhaps like this, he would have seen the body of a German officer there, nailed to a pole. He imagined the sleek breeches, the jacket neatly buttoned, the scalp glinting in the sun as the head lolled forward on the chest.

He turned to look down at the houses of Mersac. Impossible in this peaceful setting to imagine that and to grasp the implications, the horror and death that would follow. And yet . . .

for the first time he felt something disagreeable about the place, a brooding silence that he had experienced only once before in his life walking down the main street of a Welsh border town.

On his way back to the hotel he stopped at the gendarmerie. The same man was on duty; perhaps there was not enough work for two. He had his cap off today revealing short black hair glossed flat. He greeted Seagram with less reserve this time. 'Is all well, Chief Superintendent?'

'Very well.'

'I understand the girl is here?'

'Yes, I saw them both. I wonder if I could telephone Scotland Yard from your office?'

'Of course.'

To his astonishment it took the gendarme only five minutes to come up with the Yard switchboard. Seagram took the receiver. The A.C.C. was out and so was the Commissioner. He caught the scent of crisis from the voices he spoke to. Eventually one of his own sergeants, Franklin, came on the line.

'What's up?' he asked.

'Bomb – a big one. The Lord Chief Justice's country house was blown to smithereens at a quarter to nine last night.'

'Casualties?'

'None. The family are abroad and the staff are on holiday.'

He had been right then, as he sat on the hotel terrace waiting for Venniker, more right than he had imagined, scenting the wood smoke and suddenly thinking of the other sort. 'What about leads?'

'I haven't talked to anybody on the Bomb Squad. There was the usual message phoned through to the Press Association five minutes after the thing went up. First the code number and the address of the house then the words "The People Speak – no more phony justice" then "From HANGMAN". Nothing else.'

Through the open door of the gendarmerie Seagram could see a youth loading a small van with loaves. The dog who had been asleep on the cobbles the day before sat beside the van giving the youth moral support.

'Have you seen Venniker yet?' asked Franklin.

'I've seen him and he's willing to play. We're talking details later this morning. If I finish in time I may get a flight back to-night.'

'What's he doing holed up in a place like that? He wasn't exactly a country bird, was he?'

Seagram nodded as the gendarme placed a cup of coffee beside him. 'He grows things – not very well. The Château Larche is a ruin, by the way. Venniker lives in a scruffy little gate-house.' Why had he said it was scruffy, he wondered? Envy perhaps. 'Actually it's quite decent.' He looked round for milk but it seemed they were having the coffee black. 'By the way, he's become a builder.'

'What?'

'He likes building, he says. It's a hobby.'

Franklin laughed.

Yesterday's wasp was still fretting at the window where the bougainvillea arched. 'In some ways I wouldn't mind joining him.' Seagram frowned suddenly. 'I almost forgot something. The girl – Opal Rayner – I've seen her. They say they met in Rome a year ago where the man she was living with at the time had just died. She was in some sort of trouble, unspecified, and she was also short of cash. Venniker brought her back with him. Medium height, blonde, about twenty-two, very thin – could have been ill recently. Find out from the Italian police if they have anything on her. And let's see if she's carded in C.R.O.'

'Right.'

'She knows I've put a proposition to him for a job in Brussels and she also knows who I am. She says she'll keep quiet. But we've only got her word for it.'

'What did you think of her?' asked Franklin.

Seagram reflected. 'Trouble,' he said. 'Beautiful trouble.'

6

Brussels, a fat cat among cities, the cream running off its whiskers wherever Venniker looked. The taxi driver who had picked him up at the railway station drove with self-conscious formality through streets of sombre plenty, his blue cap low over his eyes. 'You're English,' he had said after two minutes' assessment.

'Yes.'

'I knew it when I saw you. *I'm* English.' He glanced briefly behind him, triumphant. The accent was American, the speech rhythm a bravado graft on some Continental base. 'My dad stayed on after World War I.' Unreal though he seemed, he was too positive to be dismissed as a joker. 'You know a town called Old*ham*? My folks lived there.'

When they reached the rue Adolphe Paul he refused to accept any tip above the levy built in by the meter. 'Give my regards to Piccadilly Circus,' he said.

Venniker reached for his grip. 'I'm afraid I can't oblige you there.' The man didn't seem to mind; saluting, brother to brother, he got back into the taxi and drove away. It was an agreeably bizarre start to the visit, perhaps auspicious.

The rue Adolphe Paul was just wide enough to contain a Rolls with a chauffeur holding the door open. It asked for little else; a street of delicate sensibilities, offering paintings, fashionable antiques and custom-built lingerie. The art dealers, Marceau Frères, stood on the corner of a square halfway along its length. The windows contained no pictures, only Chinese bowls of flowers against velvet hangings. Its door was the marvel of beaten bronze Seagram had told Venniker to look for. It opened as his foot touched the mat outside; when it closed again behind him, it gave a hiss like a giant's exhalation.

Inside, the paintings which hung on the panelled walls were

dark and medieval; one or two more, tastefully bijou, sat on easels. A man about sixty years old, watching over the treasures from a smoked glass table, rose to his feet.

'Monsieur Rezzonico?' Venniker said.

'Yes.'

'I have for sale some paintings I have been recommended to show you.'

'What sort of paintings?'

'Ikons – rather beautiful ikons.'

The man looked inscrutable. Then he indicated an inner room from which he expelled a girl to mind the store. Venniker sat in a white leather armchair beside another glass table and took the three ikons from his grip.

The man examined them with an eyeglass, placing each a long way away from him on the table as he finished with it. At the end of the performance he said, 'There has evidently been some mistake, Monsieur ...'

'Venniker.'

'Monsieur Venniker.' Monsieur Rezzonico sat back with his hands clasped, a diamond glowing discreetly on his tie. 'These are reproductions. They are quite skilfully done and there is no doubt a market for them somewhere. But in a different type of establishment.'

'You would not be interested yourself ...'

The man smiled as though he was confronted with something touching but vulgar: a chimpanzee struggling into a silk dress perhaps. 'Did you know they were reproductions, Monsieur Venniker?'

'Yes. I was not intending to ask an unreasonable price of course. Some people would presumably be quite satisfied with them.'

'No doubt.'

'Have you any suggestions?'

'Unfortunately not.'

'I see.' He stood up, reached for the ikons with a grimace. 'I won't waste any more of your time then.'

They exchanged nods of the utmost courtesy. It seemed to have gone all right. Venniker withdrew through the bronze door. From the outside, its closing sound was a thud.

He went in another taxi to drop the grip at the hotel he had booked through the accommodation bureau at the railway station, then took a walk. Seagram had provided two other addresses where he might offer the fake ikons. But it hardly seemed necessary to do it all in one afternoon. If Jewkes proved elusive he would be glad of that diversion later.

A wall plaque told him he was in Grand' Place. From the grey and gold façade of the guild houses, the stone heads of burghers looked down at the flower women's umbrellas on the cobbles beneath. Finger that filigree, the heads were saying, rap those walls, this is what we did with *our* money. Can you match that?

Promptly at six o'clock, he walked through the swing doors of the Fanton Hotel near the eastern corner of Grand' Place, carrying the ikons in a document wallet. The foyer was stone-flagged, with Persian rugs here and there so that the visitor wouldn't get too worried. A small brass plate made the sole announcement of a cocktail bar.

None of the bar stools was yet taken. Venniker selected a seat on the far curve from the door where he could hardly fail to be seen by anyone on the other stools, if not directly, then in the mirror behind the bar. Three to one you'll be lucky first time, Seagram had said; Jewkes only misses calling in if he's out of town. He likes to be seen there, occasionally picks up business of the legitimate sort – his bamboo stuff. We know he's around at the moment. Give it three nights running anyway, the drinks are on the Queen. Venniker ordered a Chivas Regal.

A dozen others had joined him, either at the bar or at the tables behind, before he sensed rather than saw that perhaps Seagram had got the odds right. Someone of exactly the right specification was taking the bar stool by the door; but as he tried to look, the barman moved across his line of sight. Bending into the light of the lamp on the bar top, he offered his profile and waited.

It took a minute or two. A vodka martini was being mixed by the barman although Venniker hadn't heard it being ordered. He was conscious that the muscles in his cheek had begun to tighten. He decided he would have to shift his position. Then a hand reached across, squeezed his forearm very gently as though testing for ripeness. Chunky rings adorned three of the fingers; the cuticles had had a lot of care. 'Paul Venniker!' a voice said, rather huskier than he had expected, tending to mid-Atlantic but with Willesden not quite extinguished.

Venniker looked sideways, let his face relax slowly, the lower lip dropping, a smile stealing up to rescue it at the last moment.

'Moley!'

Always well covered even in less prosperous days, Jewkes was not just plump now but as fat a cat as Brussels itself. His tailor had faced the problems as best he could. The safari suit in pale blue denim with a longer than average jacket was cut straight and sat as smoothly as worsted wool. Gone, far gone, as though it had never been, the Weaver to Wearer double-breasted chalk-stripe of the Bedgley bucket shop days. A whole new philosophy of dress had taken over – a wisp of Hermes at the throat, a silver band about the wrist, on the feet basket-weave shoes the same colour as the suit. A soft leather handbag for the things that might have spoiled the line of the suit was on the bar top. If it wasn't exactly *le style jet*, Moley was right up there with the beautiful ones.

They reminisced. Wonderingly, Jewkes went back to Bedgley and the days before civilization embraced him. He was fond if muzzy. Now and then he rolled a finger and thumb affectionately inside a curly grey beard; he was being understanding about his old self. It took two more vodka martinis before he got round to asking Venniker what he was doing in Brussels.

'Trying to sell a few paintings.'

'Art?'

'Ikons.'

'Ikons! I always said you had class, Paul!' He squeezed Venniker's forearm again, a very warm human being. 'What's wrong with the London market?'

'I don't live there now. I moved to France some years ago. I live in a fairly remote part of the Lot.'

'The quiet life,' said Jewkes. 'And why not, for God's sake?'

'When I saw the big property boys moving over here I reckoned that was the writing on the wall. So I came.'

'Is that your line now – property?'

'Not altogether.' Jewkes was inspecting a newly-arrived girl at the other end of the bar. It was obvious he wanted to change the subject. 'You solo, Paul?'

'Here, yes. There's a girl back in France.'

'One to one,' said Jewkes. 'That's nice. One to one relationships are best, Paul. Take that from me.' He looked at the watch face on the inside of his wrist. 'Hang on and you'll meet my chick.' He took an olive; the lips moved moistly within their curly grey fastness. 'You'll like Dewi.' Wherever it was he had been going in his life, he clearly wanted it to be known that he was there.

They had gone back to talking about prison by the time Dewi arrived. Jewkes recalled Bedgley rather as though it had been a place of retreat providing the key to self-knowledge. Money, he was saying, money is important, Paul, my God it is. But it's like a woman, you've got to make as though you don't love it so much you can't let it go. Then it always finds a way back. He was settling into the guru role when the girl made her entrance. Olive-skinned, with loose black hair, dressed in unbuttoned shirt and sharkskin pants, she was a genuine showstopper. She moved slowly, undulating with care as though on a 1940's film staircase. 'One thing, Paul,' said Jewkes when she was still making the approach, 'the name is Rex. Rex Arundel.'

'Fine,' Venniker said, 'fine, Rex.' They laughed, old comrades from when girls were only pictures on the wall.

Jewkes rose to nuzzle Dewi. 'Baby.' As he kissed the inside of her palm, she tossed her hair and let her eyes go round the room so that the others could be sure of what they were missing. When he introduced Venniker, 'A friend from way back, baby,' she looked at him as she might at a mirror, parting her lips and tilting her head a little way. They had exchanged about twenty words before she was up and gone again, to make telephone calls for which Jewkes provided small coins.

'This place of yours,' Jewkes said, watching her buttocks negotiate the doorway, 'you say it's remote. How far from the nearest town?'

'The nearest real town is Cahors – about sixty kilometres.'

'Are you on a main route?'

'No, quite a long way off.'

'And it's just you and the chick?'

'That's right.'

'Great.' He was playing another role now, something to do with Love and Nature and the Real Things in Life. 'I really go for that.' After a pause he went on. 'And the art stuff – tell me about it.'

'I've got some here ...' Venniker looked round and pointed to an empty table. When they were seated he took the ikons from the document wallet and showed them to Jewkes. 'These are done by an Italian I sometimes work with. The standard is pretty high. A lot have been sold to Japanese and American collectors. I'd been tipped off that a dealer called Rezzonico who's got a place called Marceau Frères in rue Adolphe Paul didn't have any objection to the odd fake. But he was too suspicious when I turned up today, presumably because he's never met me before. Anyway he took the line he never handled fakes. That was rather a blow. If you know anybody in the game who would buy, I'd appreciate your putting in a word. I need the bread pretty badly.'

Jewkes was curling his beard round the little finger of his left hand. 'No outlet in France?'

'The market's nervous there since someone sued a dealer in Paris last year.'

Jewkes lit a menthol. 'I'd like to help, Paul. The problem is that it's not quite my territory.'

'Then can you plug me into anything else? You know me well enough.'

'*Anything?*'

'Anything.'

'I'm not sure ...' He was thinking about it all the same. 'Are you in Brussels a while?'

'I'll give it two or three days. There are a few other dealers I'm going to try.'

'Where are you staying?'

'The Pierre Bonnard. It's a small hotel near the railway station.'

Jewkes' lips rounded, emitted smoke in judicial deliberation. 'O.K. If I have any ideas I'll leave a message for you there.'

It was impossible to be sure he meant it. But he wrote the hotel's name in a pocket diary. He also asked the name of the man at Marceau Frères again.

When Dewi finally got back from her telephone calls, he had begun to look a shade less benevolent. He thrust her drink into her hand and held out the wrist with the watch on it. 'Baby, we've got to run. We'll drop Paul off at his hotel – it's on the way.' He hadn't asked Venniker if he wanted to leave yet.

They drove to the hotel in an open Cadillac. Dewi's hair streamed behind as their banner, her nipples sculptured rosettes on the silk shirt, profile lifted slightly for the proles to marvel at. She spoke only cnce. 'My headscarf,' she said, 'in the glove box, lover.'

Venniker stood at the kerb after they had dropped him and waited while she adjusted the scarf. A handsome pair in their way, cocooned in technology, bright with baubles, they looked immune to disease, debts, the *longueurs* of the one-to-one as others might know it. But how could that be? Jewkes was looking up as he swung the wheel. 'Blessings, Paul.' Then they were gone.

He ate a meal in the restaurant next to the hotel before going to his bedroom to telephone the number Seagram had given him. He was answered by a female voice. Seagram was not there. He felt slight irritation that Seagram had not been standing by for news of progress.

'What message shall I give him?' the woman asked. She sounded the notebook and sharpened pencil type.

'Just tell him I met my friend tonight and there may be more developments tomorrow.'

She repeated it back. 'I'll ask him to telephone you as soon as he gets in.'

'No,' he said, 'I'm going to bed. Tell him I'll be in touch again.'

He wondered who she was. Obviously English, although her French accent when she picked up the phone had been quite smooth. Perhaps she was a policewoman brought over from the Yard to answer Seagram's telephone and to take down his great thoughts. Or she might be an Embassy secretary press-ganged into service; but somehow he couldn't see Seagram showing his hand to the diplomats in order to get help for this operation.

While he was at the telephone he decided to ring Opal. She took a long time answering. When the receiver was eventually picked up at the other end, the line was so full of crackling and general noise, he could only just make out her words.

'How are you?' he asked.

'Fine.'

'Are you eating?'

'All the time. Aldo shot a rabbit yesterday. I'm going to try cooking it. We shall have it for lunch tomorrow – if I get it right.'

He couldn't begin to imagine that. 'What else is happening?'

'Nothing. What about you? Are you having fun?'

'I wouldn't call it that.'

Suddenly he knew what the noise behind the crackling was: beat music. Opal must have the player turned up to maximum volume in the bedroom. 'That record player is bloody loud.'

'Having it loud helps.'

'Helps what?'

'Being alone.'

'I'll be back soon,' he said.

'Don't worry, it's not that bad.'

He wished he could see her face, to judge how bad it really was. But it was no good worrying at this distance.

Seagram came through when he was already in bed. He was bloated with optimism. 'First time lucky! Congratulations.'

Wearily he said, 'I left a message that I'd contact you tomorrow. Didn't your . . .'

Seagram wasn't listening. 'Did he say he'd find you a piece of the action?'

'Just that he'd see if he could help. He was very close about what he did. And I can't contact him – we're dependent on him telephoning me.'

'But you're hopeful. I mean – you re-established a relationship with him. Old friends . . .'

'More or less. But he's a fantasy figure now. He's invented a new personality for himself.'

'No more caramel toffees.'

'Perhaps when he's alone. It's difficult to take him seriously. Or dislike him.'

Seagram said, 'He's a syphilitic fat bastard living off the proceeds of persuading people to inject themselves into an early grave and playing along with a bunch of nuts who can't think of anything better to do than blow us all up.'

Venniker smiled into the receiver. 'How do you know he's syphilitic?'

'Never mind. I've got to fly to London tomorrow afternoon but I hope to be back early the next day. You can always get a message to me through this number.'

There was one other call before he was finally able to sleep. A female voice speaking French that was better than that of Seagram's sidekick but still not quite perfect, asked, 'Is that Monsieur Venniker?'

'Yes.'

'Forgive me for troubling you. It is a question of your full address in France. Can you give it to me, please.'

Some bureaucratic inquiry from the hotel's reception desk, he thought, in his half-asleep state; they couldn't read his registration card.

'Château Larche, Mersac, Lot.'

Doubt swelled as she read it back.

'Who is this?' he asked.

There was a pause and then the line went dead. The hotel telephone operator said it was an outside call.

7

Morning broke under a sky unwaveringly grey and heavy. From his window the city seemed like an unlit room after sunblinding days at Larche. There was no break in the cloud base as the day wore on; and no telephone call from Jewkes.

Venniker smoked more cigarettes before lunch than for five years. Imperceptibly to himself, he had moved from a calculating acceptance of a role to be performed and paid for to a stance of irritable commitment. He wanted success. He wanted to prove something to Seagram. He wanted to prove it to himself.

By six o'clock he had begun to think of looking for Jewkes again in the bar of the Hotel Fanton. But the plan he had agreed with Seagram required that he should never seem to make the running. He searched the Brussels telephone directory for a Jewkes or an Arundel but there was none. Finally, he went out, carrying the document wallet with the ikons inside, telling himself he would at least keep his cover alive by trying them on another dealer. But when he got to the next shop on the list Seagram had supplied, it was closed.

No reasonably direct route back could take him past the Fanton but he found himself there all the same. On the other side of the street, he smoked yet another cigarette and watched cars drive up to the entrance. Then he cursed himself for childishness and stupidity and returned to the Pierre Bonnard, convinced now of failure.

But as he entered the foyer and saw the reception clerk reach towards the letter rack, he knew all was not yet lost.

The letter was typewritten on plain paper without a heading. Retreating behind the plastic replica of the Manikin Pis on the corner of the reception counter he read it quickly.

Paul, I may have something for you. I suggest we meet at the Café Joseph on the corner of rue des Bouchers and rue Dobrai at eight-thirty. Please make sure you come on foot and walk along the rue Dobrai to get there.

It was signed with the letter 'R' which he concluded after a while stood for Rex. It certainly wasn't the sort of letter the old Moley would have written. This was Rex Arundel at large in the world of affairs. He looked across at the clerk. 'Who delivered this?'

'A taxi driver. He brought it a few minutes after you went out.'

Venniker was half-way along the rue Dobrai when he fathomed the significance of the final sentence of the letter. The open Cadillac purred alongside him. Jewkes said in a very mid-Atlantic voice, 'Come aboard, Paul.'

Jewkes was wearing a Breton cap of pale blue suede. There was no Dewi this time. Venniker got in beside him. 'Did you think I might get lost?'

Jewkes laughed. 'A little precaution. My employers are rather fanatical about security. We're not in fact going to the Café Joseph but to the Café Grand' Place. If you haven't been there, it's worth a look.'

He swung the Cadillac round a couple of blocks and almost at once they were in the great square surrounded by the guild houses. Coloured lights picked out the gold leaf on the cornices, the gilded head of a cardinal. The flower sellers had gone home and Bach was being played very softly over the loudspeakers. 'Tourist stuff,' said Jewkes as they climbed out of the Cadillac in one corner of the square. 'It's a difficult town to sell. They try.'

They sat at an upstairs table in the café. A stuffed horse guarded the stairway and pigs' bladders hung from a smoky ceiling. Most of the seats were occupied by students and the noise level was high. An elderly man wearing a high stiff collar and *pince nez* was holding the hand of a sulky boy very tightly. Against the wall in the corner nearest to the table Jewkes had chosen, there was a solitary girl with cropped black hair reading a newspaper.

'Any luck with the ikons?' asked Jewkes after they had ordered drinks. He had kept the Breton cap on.

'No.'

'I'm sorry.'

'Your note . . .'

'I've nothing in the art line Paul. But if you'd consider something a little different.'

'You know the answer to that.'

'It might even be very lucrative. Put it this way; if you can do one job well there may be more gravy in the pan.'

'That would be nice.'

'One thing.' Jewkes rolled a finger in his beard as though it was a very delicate operation. 'You've no hang-ups about jobs?'

'Not if they're reasonably safe. What do I have to do?'

'A delivery. Somebody has been wanting to do business with my employers for some time. But they needed to check him out before going ahead. Now something has to be handed over as soon as possible. It's already been paid for.'

'Where does he live?'

'In Brussels.'

'If it's as close as that, why do you need somebody like me to make the delivery?'

'Security. Although the first delivery in this business is always in person they don't allow the purchaser to go on meeting anyone in the main organization. He's had contact with me but that's over now. You've been living in France for years and before that you were in England. We believe this guy's never been to either place. So there's no chance of your having met and no likelihood of your ever meeting again. That's the way we want it.'

The girl in the corner had put her newspaper down and was impassively watching the elderly man trying to get the boy out of his sulks. Her jaw was perhaps on the square side but there was nothing else wrong with her appearance. She was in an uncompromising way very beautiful.

'Are you going to tell me what I'm delivering?'

'It's a box of samples of Belgian glass. The packing in the middle of the box contains something else. You don't have to worry about that.'

'But how do we know for sure I'm not walking into some sort of trap? This man – you haven't dealt with him before. He could be a police agent.'

Jewkes stared into his glass. 'His address will be under observation for four hours before you visit him. And he doesn't know exactly when the delivery is being made – only that he's got to wait at home for it. If there's any sign of a trap you'll be warned in time to stop you entering the building. All that's involved for you once you get there is to hand the purchaser the package together with a letter which you must see he opens first. It will give him instructions about where he is to deposit money if he wants another delivery next week and where the next package will be hidden – because all later deliveries will be by that system. After you leave him spend not less than one hour on the move, making sure you've not been followed by anyone. Then you can go back to your hotel.'

'What is this organization? Who am I working for? And where do you fit in? Can't you tell me a bit more?'

Jewkes gave his sympathetic smile. 'Be patient and take my word that you're in on a good thing. Later on you may get to meet somebody else who'll tell you more.'

The Café Grand' Place was filling. Up the stairs came trudging a dogged band of American senior citizens, momentarily loose from culture's chains to drink an atmospheric lager. A student with almost white hair and transparent-framed spectacles weaved his way through them as they paused to study the stuffed horse and finally sat down at the girl's table, snapping his fingers until the waiter came. But they apparently weren't together; after staring at the newcomer once the girl turned her eyes towards Venniker. He couldn't make up his mind whether he saw a hint of inquiry in them.

Jewkes said, 'Do you accept the deal?'

'Yes. Where's the package?'

'That'll be delivered to your hotel tomorrow with two letters – one for the customer, as I said, and one for you with the address and other details you'll need. In the meantime there's nothing for you to do. This is on account.' Jewkes took some bank notes from an envelope and handed them over. They were Swiss francs, five hundred in tens, very clean.

'I'll leave you now, Paul. Stay ten more minutes before you leave yourself. To be on the safe side.' Plump fingers crept over Venniker's forearm, squeezed. 'We'll be in touch.'

He stayed in his seat as Jewkes had asked. Three Belgians took the remaining places at the table. Venniker looked across at the girl in the corner. Her eye met his and stayed long enough for him to be sure now that she was interested, coolly perhaps, but interested anyway. She was older than he had first thought, twenty-seven or eight. Idly he played with the thought of picking her up How long was it since he had picked anyone up? He would need to think back to the days before Faith Beswick and he wasn't going to do that. Banal phrases of greeting stumbled through his brain and collapsed under a barrage of ridicule. And after dinner, supposing they came to the point, how would he put it? Sorry, I should warn you, there's a problem I've been having lately, a little local difficulty, I can't guarantee . . . Somehow he couldn't hear himself saying any of it; not with the hard-eyed student with white hair listening to his opening spiel.

He went down the stairs without glancing at the girl again. Walking across Grand' Place, he told himself he ought to pass a message on progress to the telephone number Seagram had given him. But he was gripped by a growing melancholy. The fact that Jewkes had swallowed the hook no longer meant anything. In a restaurant on rue des Dominicains he tackled a *bifteck et frites* dispiritedly and watched the tourists. He knew he needed to do something positive to help to shake off the mood. A theatre for culture, perhaps? Or a brothel for therapy? But he had no inclination towards anything. He pushed the *bifteck* away and concentrated on his bottle of wine. He had drunk enough to be sure of being slightly drunk when he left the restaurant. About him, as he walked back to his hotel, people appeared like marionettes, jerking and lunging across his path in meaningless pursuits. In his hotel he undressed with difficulty, looked again at the Swiss banknotes to satisfy himself they weren't Monopoly money and fell asleep almost at once.

The package was delivered to his hotel the next afternoon while he was sitting in the gardens of the Royal Palace counting the catastrophes, current and imminent, that *Le Monde* had notched up for its readers. He wondered if his departure had been watched so that he would be unable to intercept and interrogate the messenger who brought it. The accompanying letter contained a sealed envelope addressed to Mr Jack Ebner and typed instructions for himself. He was to take the package to Ebner at a flat on the third floor, 14 rue Marcelis, arriving precisely at eight o'clock, to wait while Ebner read the letter and then to leave. He was to make sure he was not followed either going to or coming away; if he was, he must take effective evasive action and if he was still carrying the package, hide it. Finally he was to go back to the hotel and wait. There was no signature but a further sentence at the bottom telling him to burn the note when he had memorized it.

He put the note in the lining of this grip together with the previous one; Seagram might be able to get something out of them in the way of clues. When the time arrived to start out, he took a conscientious half an hour in and around the Galeries St Hubert making sure he was clean. Everything looked all right but he still used a couple of taxis for the last leg.

The address was a small apartment block with a tiled entrance hall and an elevator that had stone steps to one side. From the doorway, Venniker glanced back to the street. It was deserted except for two women exchanging gossip, a bored Sealyham terrier at their feet, and a dark-skinned boy in tight pants waiting on a corner for Prince Charming to come along.

He avoided the elevator and walked up to the third floor. The doors of two apartments stood side by side, each with cardboard notices on them. The left-hand notice said: *Soyez gentil de ne faire aucun bruit – il y a un bébé qui est malade*. The other was shorter: *The Ebner Ranch*, it announced. Venniker pressed the bell.

There was no response at first. He tried a longer burst and placed his head against the door. Faintly he heard the creak of a bed and feet hitting the floor. Whoever was home on the ranch had been in the bunkhouse. A man opened the door on a chain and looked out through the crack. He was pale and thin-faced, with shoulder-length hair and a bad case of acne.

'Ebner?'

'Could be.'

'I have a package for you.'

The man looked over Venniker's shoulder.

'Just me,' Venniker said.

The chain was taken off its hook. Suitcases and hold-alls littered the margins of a very small hall. They went into a sitting-room that was no tidier. A few posters and photographs had been taped on to the walls, some jokey, some macabre. One photograph was of a young black woman in spectacles whose features he vaguely recalled seeing in newspapers, another of policemen with large stomachs beating up youths. There was also a dollar bill on which Chairman Mao's face had been substituted for that of George Washington.

Ebner picked up a bottle of Jack Daniels from the floor. He looked about twenty-five and well over the hill; but slowly he was winding himself up to be hospitable. 'Excuse the mess but nobody cleans this place.' He ferreted out two empty yoghourt cups from behind a pile of news magazines. 'Drink?'

'Thank you.'

'We haven't met.'

'No.'

'I'd say you're English.'

Venniker watched the Jack Daniels covering an earlier tide mark in one of the cups. 'Right.'

'But you live here in Brussels . . . ?'

'No, France.'

'France! I didn't know the organization had a set-up there.'

Venniker smiled and drank, letting it ride. 'I have to give you these.' He handed over the envelope and the package.

Ebner sat on the edge of a table holding them. He was wearing a pink shirt with a frilly front and half-unzipped jeans. 'How is it in France?'

He shrugged.

'Does Françoise get down there?'

'I wouldn't know, I'm afraid.'

'But you've met her?'

'No.'

Ebner looked thoughtful. 'Who then?'

He felt he had to say something. 'Rex.'

'Rexy.' Ebner's expression was disappointed. 'Yeah.' He looked in his yoghourt cup. 'I guessed I might get to see Françoise this time. Doesn't she want to know who she's doing business with?'

'Perhaps you'd open the letter. I'm told it explains everything.'

Venniker watched Ebner read it. 'O.K.' he said shortly. He refolded the paper carefully and put it back in the envelope; he was a shade more reserved. Raising his drink to Venniker, he said, 'Well, thanks.' He showed no sign of wanting to open the package.

Venniker pointed. 'If you'd check the contents . . .'

'Not necessary.' Ebner drained his cup and watched Venniker's hand until Venniker raised it and finished his own drink. 'Well, thanks again . . .'

'. . . Paul.'

'Paul.'

Venniker paused on the way out by the photograph of policemen swinging clubs. 'Daley's pogrom,' said Ebner.

Venniker shook his head. 'What?'

'The Democratic Convention in Chicago. You never heard of that?'

'Vaguely. Are you in the photograph?' He peered into the faces of the youths.

'No.'

'But you have a reason . . .?'

'I was around,' Ebner said vaguely. He crossed the hall and opened the apartment door. 'So long, Paul. See you again maybe.' From the next apartment came the sound of a baby crying. 'Jesus Christ, not again,' he said and shut the door.

Venniker placed an ear against the panels. It seemed as though the baby was going to make it pointless but obligingly it began to choke and had to pause for breath. Behind the door the telephone Venniker had noticed in Ebner's hall was being dialled. There was a brief silence then Ebner's voice, sounding urgent, said, 'Look, it's happened, a guy just called and made the delivery.' There was another silence before he went on, 'How in Christ could I know?' Finally, he said, 'O.K., O.K. I'll take a look.'

Venniker went down the stairs two at a time. In the street the boy in tight pants was still looking into the distance for his beau. The rear of the Sealyham was disappearing into the apartment block on the other side of the street. If anything the area was more peaceful than when he had arrived.

He was twenty or thirty yards away from 14, rue Marcelis,

when the explosion erupted behind him. He knew instantaneously its meaning, knew everything from how it happened to what it would have done; even so, he couldn't bring himself to accept the fact.

When he looked back he saw glass and the shattered frame of a window on the pavement; above, on the third floor of the apartment house he had just left, smoke and dust poured from a gaping hole. Crossing the street, he stared upwards. From a lower corner of the hole something hung as though on display, a piece of meat, dressed as to one half of it in frilly pink material. His eyes clung to it, trying unsuccessfully to work out what part of Ebner it had constituted. Finally he turned and moved jerkily down the street. His eyes now remained on the pavement. Within him there was a stone, a boulder, growing larger every second.

He was in an area of snug burgher tranquillity and had been walking for over five minutes, when abruptly he knew it was hopeless to struggle against the turmoil inside him. Almost thankfully he was sick against a creepered wall.

8

Moving from bar to bar, as though a series of different atmospheres might somehow combine to detach him from what had gone before, he steadily drank cognac until it burned his guts. After the earlier sickness, he had felt no nausea. Somewhere he could not afterwards recall, he ate a sandwich to find out if he could actually do it, swallowing the final sawdust crumbs in grim triumph.

From the second of the bars he had put through a call to Seagram's number. The secretary bird told him that Seagram had been delayed in London but was on his way back.

'When does he get in?'

'I can't tell you.'

He ground his teeth. 'Then bloody well find out.'

She became injured. 'If you have a message I shall give it to him as soon as . . .'

'How do you know he isn't still in his office at the Yard?'

'Because he telephoned me when he was leaving for the airport.'

He gave up. 'All right. But tell him this, I'll be in the Cathedral at ten tomorrow morning. If he doesn't show up, I'm taking the first train out.'

'The Cathedral,' she said. 'I'm not sure . . .'

He had faintly remembered passing it, on his way back from the Palace gardens during the afternoon. 'If I can find it, he can. And tell him I'm out for the night.'

He meant it then but not later, when weariness began to overpower the liquor. As he made his way, still too sober, to his hotel, there was a hint of rain in the air. He would have welcomed a storm, a typhoon, anything that would tear the place apart. But he walked more slowly now, getting his control back; anyone seeing him would have supposed he was relaxed, a handsome man with a southern tan, roaming through the night at a loose end.

In his room the curtains had been drawn and the lamp by the bed was on. Well away from the lamp, seated in the only arm-chair, was someone smoking a cigarette. The face was in deep shadow but he could see from the hand holding the ash tray on a thigh that it was a woman. When he pressed the switch for the centre light, it was like being asked to face a fantasy sought and then abandoned a long time ago.

It was the girl with cropped black hair who had sat in the café on the Grand' Place. 'Well, well,' he said. It seemed a fairly safe thing to say.

'Welcome back.'

Venniker leaned against the door. 'How exactly did you get in?'

'A little trick I learned once.' The voice was English.

'Where?'

'Does it matter?'

'Yes.'

'In South America.' The girl stubbed out the cigarette and placed the ash tray on the bedside table in a neat movement that took in brushing some ash from the thigh. 'You remember me?'

'I remember you.'

He sat down on the bed to study her. She was even more beautiful this close; long legs, a bust that was small but high, a smooth white skin so cool in all its planes that the strong jaw seemed of no account in the final analysis. She wore a cotton shirt dress that was just smart enough. On the floor by her side was a large shoulder bag.

'What I'd like to know,' he said, 'is who the hell you are?'

'I'm Françoise.'

'Françoise.' The taste of the cognac was sour in his mouth. He got up and drew a glass of water from the tap in the bathroom and dropped in two Alka Seltzers. 'Françoise what?' he called.

'Just Françoise.'

Tablets and memory suddenly fizzed together. He saw Ebner's face over the yoghourt cup in the apartment on the rue Marcelis. I guessed I might get to see Françoise this time, Ebner was saying. *Well Ebner, she's here. Just a little bit too late for you.*

He went back into the bedroom. 'Now I understand.'

'Do you?'

'Ebner mentioned your name.'

She raised an eyebrow as though it was mildly interesting.

'Of course you know what happened to Ebner?'

'Yes, of course I know.'

'Why couldn't I be warned that I wasn't just delivering drugs to him?'

'Why should you have even thought you were?'

He frowned. 'What?'

'Taking drugs to him.'

It was a slip; he covered up by looking angry. 'That was the general idea I got from Arundel.'

'Rex never said anything like that.'

'Nor did he say it was murder.'

'You told him you were ready for anything.'

'I'd have liked to have the choice.'

She picked up the shoulder bag. 'We decided you wouldn't feel better if you knew. And you'd certainly act more calmly as things were.' Her voice had no particular accent but he guessed her background to be middle class: a Sloane Ranger gone rogue, perhaps. 'Anyway, why be upset? You're no more responsible for what happened than the postman who delivers a letter bomb.' There was a roll of bank notes in her hand; she counted them out on to the bed in front of him, five thousand Swiss francs. 'Thank you for a good job.'

He took off his jacket and lay back against the bed board with his eyes closed. 'If I'd been there another five minutes you'd have been spared the expense.'

'The letter to Ebner which you handed over said you were not authorized to see what was in the package and he was on no account to open it until you'd left. We were quite sure you'd be safe before he triggered the detonator.'

'Did he have to be killed in such a messy way?'

'He was an agent of the American Government who'd managed to establish a relationship with us. He knew we were into drugs and asked for a supply. While we were checking on him we discovered he was paying visits to the house of the top man in the American Drugs Enforcement Office here.' She pushed fingers through her hair; it was the first sign he had seen of anything approaching tension. 'When that sort of thing happens it's important to make it clear we can deal with traitors.'

'How could you know the entrance to the apartment house wasn't being watched by the Americans? They could have followed me afterwards.'

'You were told to be on the look-out.'

'But not about the extent of the risk.'

'There was somebody nearby. We made sure you were clean.' Françoise moved to the bed and sat down beside him. 'Just as we didn't want you blown up and took precautions against it, so we would have made sure you weren't caught by the Americans or the Belgian police or anybody. You can trust us – we're quite efficient.'

'*We?*'

She placed her hand lightly on his leg. 'Why don't you stop worrying?' Her expression was cool, a little clinical; but her hand stayed there. 'How do you feel now?'

'Wary.'

'Are you still with us?'

'I might be. As long as the money matches the risk – and I know what I'm being asked to do.'

She was studying him as though to be quite sure the face read the same way as the words. Her fingers counted themselves against the flesh of his thighs, one, two, three, four, and again very slowly. It was not unpleasant but ambiguous. Finally she took the hand away and held it towards him to shake. 'Here's to the future, Paul.'

She sat back and lit another cigarette. Her movements were exceptionally crisp, as though each had been planned ahead for economy and exact timing. Venniker said, 'I take it Françoise isn't your real name?'

She smiled a quick miserly smile he had noted before. 'I just happen to like it.' She had an assurance about her that could make her beauty a rather neutral thing.

'And you're English.'

'Yes.'

'That's almost the first thing you've told me about yourself. Am I going to learn any more or have I got to put up with working with a code name?'

'My real name is irrelevant. You'll find out what really matters about me soon enough.' She began to prowl the room. 'This place of yours in France. It's a ruin in the middle of nowhere, I gather.'

He nodded, trying to remember if he had told Jewkes it was a ruin; but he probably had.

'I'm interested because we need somewhere like that. A quiet country place. To store things.'

'But if you're operating from Brussels, what use is a store in the Lot? Larche is hundreds of miles away.'

'It's a different operation I'm thinking about. The goods become available near Paris. Your place would meet the requirements quite well.' She stubbed out the cigarette. 'I also have a special reason for liking the idea of the Lot.'

He thought she might go on to explain herself. Instead she said, 'The storage would have to be four or five times the size of this room and dry.'

'There's a tunnel or cellar which is reasonably dry. Would that suit?'

'It could be ideal.'

'It's really an underground passage. It once connected the main house with a *pigeonnier* which I've rebuilt. The far end of the passage has fallen in but the rest of it is usable. I cleared it out last year – it was a wine store as well. The only entrance now is from inside the *pigeonnier* – there's a door that could be locked.'

'Who else knows about it?'

'The man who helps me with the land. But he has no reason to go in there. He wouldn't be the slightest bit interested if I kept it locked. Also the girl who lives with me.'

Françoise stopped by the light switch at the door, and flicked it off, leaving just the bedside lamp burning. 'What's her name?'

'Opal.'

'We should want Opal to move on.'

'I see,' he said. 'And supposing I didn't . . .'

She stopped frowning and smiled; she was being as conciliatory as her nature seemed likely to allow. 'We could talk about that.'

'Apart from which,' he went on, 'I still have to decide that the risk is worth taking.'

'I promise you it's worth more than anything you've ever done in your life. In every way.'

Somebody walked along the corridor outside and paused at the door of the bedroom. A key tried the lock and stuck. Françoise moved swiftly to grab her shoulder bag and reach inside it, then positioned herself beside the hinges of the door. The key tried again. There was a curse outside. After a pause the footsteps moved on to the next door and the key turned at last.

'That was a very interesting performance,' he said. 'Do you always carry a gun?'

'Almost always. There are risks in our business. I don't believe in being unprepared.' She dropped the gun back in the bag. 'If the occasional car or truck came to your place at night would it be noticed from nearby houses?'

'There aren't any houses that near. Anyway odd cars are always turning in and going away again – tourists make the mistake of thinking there's a château to be looked at. Such locals as there are take no notice.'

Françoise nodded; she was frowning again as she thought. 'I ought to visit and see for myself.' She pursed her lips. 'The Château Larche, Mersac . . . Sounds impressive.'

Venniker caught an echo. 'It was you who telephoned my room the night I ran into Arundel, wasn't it?'

'Yes.'

'Checking, I suppose – just as you sat watching me in the Café Grand' Place.'

'I was also listening to what you said in the Café.'

'From that distance?'

'Yes.'

He laughed. 'Don't tell me Arundel had a microphone in that cap.'

She shrugged; obviously it didn't strike her as much of a joke. She was standing by the bed, looking down at Venniker. 'At first I wondered if you were queer.'

'What did you decide in the end?'

'That you weren't. But that you might be rather cool. Are you cool?'

'It depends on the weather.'

Placing a hand on his shoulder, she kissed his mouth. Her breath was very clean even after the cigarettes. He gave as good as he received. When she lifted her head she was not quite as calm as she had been before.

He took her hand from his shoulder and looked at the palm and the nails; to his surprise they were bitten hard. 'What are you thinking?' she asked.

'I was wondering if you packed the explosive yourself.'

She didn't mind; it was also obvious that she was confident he didn't mind either. She kissed him again. It was both accomplished and predatory. 'More checking?' he said.

'There are worse ways of finding out about a man. My experience is that it's surprisingly reliable.'

She was starting to undress. He said, 'I ought to warn you we may strike a problem.' So here he was, saying it after all.

'What sort of problem?'

Suddenly, watching her, he didn't believe what he was saying. He shook his head. 'Never mind.'

She lay on the bed beside him unbuttoning his shirt. He had a fleeting sensation of being prepared for an urgent operation. Doubt returned briefly until he looked at her mouth. Then no problem at all.

Afterwards, while she smoked a cigarette, he tried to think about the implications. Perhaps it was nothing more complicated than a change of sensation, somebody fresh. But there was another possibility. This relationship was neutral – no obligations, no emotional ties and vibrations. It was as isolated an event of his physical life as anything he could think of. Once, back in the time when Faith Beswick was keeping him, he had feared he would one day have nothing left to offer except a performance – no tenderness, no love, no giving other than as a piece of theatre. Perhaps that had been the truth all along. His sexual integrity was all right if there were no complications; grafted on to something more abstract, it sickened and fell apart.

'No problem,' Françoise said.

'No.'

She placed the cigarette between his lips. 'You're quite something.'

He listened to her heart beating against his side.

'You know that, of course. That you're very accomplished.'

'Once upon a time I took it rather seriously. I had to.'

She laughed. It was the first time he had heard her laugh. 'Why?'

He hesitated; but there was no reason not to tell her. 'I did a spell in prison once. When I came out I went through a very bad patch. I had no confidence I could succeed in anything. Except this. You could say it was what kept me going.'

Listen, Faith Beswick had said, we're going to talk cash. I'm finding the money for you to buy that club. There'll also be a quarterly payment into the bank – to help with the rates and taxes. That's all. We're never going to mention this again because I don't choose to think about it. It's not relevant to why you spend time with me, why you can't get enough of me. But not only can't you get enough of me, you're going to keep on telling me that all the time. And I'm going to believe it. Is that understood, darling?

He returned the cigarette to Françoise's mouth. 'I got into a long-term arrangement with a particular woman. She kept me on what was a reasonably considerate basis. Then something happened – it was nothing to do with the relationship, a girl who lived upstairs and was on drugs was killed. I decided to get away. That was my retirement from being a stud. End of autobiography.'

She began to stroke his body without looking at him. 'Well, well.' He could tell that in addition to being amused she was mildly stirred. He made her turn her face towards him. 'Don't I deserve to know something about you now?'

'Not yet.'

'Why should the rules be different on your side?'

'There's more at stake on my side. One day I may be able to trust you.'

'Do you trust anybody?'

She considered. 'There are two people I trust. My safety is in their hands – I've had to accept that. I believe they won't let me down unless they're in extremity – like being tortured. Nobody is trustworthy in every circumstance.'

'What more have you got to find out about me before we reach that stage of trust?'

'How much staying-power you've got. Your attitude towards things like society, politics, money.'

He laughed. 'Why should my attitude to any of those be relevant to my being trustworthy?'

She stubbed out the cigarette. 'We'll talk about it one day. Not now.'

When he awoke, it was full daylight outside. Françoise was still asleep beside him. He began to wonder whether he was going to get away for the meeting he had arranged with Seagram. He had dropped into a doze again when he felt her sliding out of the bed. Through half-closed eyes he saw flesh shimmering away into the bathroom. The door was closed, in a moment he heard the bath taps running.

Straining his ears he just caught the splash as she got into the tub. Her clothing was on the armchair but the bag that had contained the revolver was nowhere to be seen; she must have taken it into the bathroom with her. He cursed and went over to examine the clothing. The labels were Belgian and English; there were no laundry marks. The pocket of the dress contained a ticket stub for the Curzon Cinema in London. There was also a scrap of cellophane from a cigarette pack. But not a hint of a clue which could lead to identifying her.

He was back between the sheets, trying the radio for a news bulletin when she reappeared. 'I'll order coffee,' he said. 'Come back to bed.'

'No.' She was putting on pants in a brisk, fairly inelegant way. 'I have to go.' The party was over.

'Why the hurry?'

'I have to fix the details of a trip I'm making. Can you stay in Brussels for a day or two?'

'Why?'

'It would suit us. We'd contact you here.'

'I don't think I want to hang about in this town.'

'We'd pay your expenses of course.'

He could imagine Seagram's voice in his ear, urging him to

agree, also offering expenses ... But he wasn't having it. 'No, I have to get back to Larche tomorrow. There are things to be done.'

Françoise looked at him impatiently, then glanced at her wristwatch and shrugged. 'Perhaps it's all the same. We can get in touch with you there if we decide to look at your place.'

She moved to the bed, buttoning her dress. The night had left her unmarked by either satiety or fatigue. She bent down. 'Take care.' She wasn't vulnerable now. But nor was her kiss just polite.

When the door closed behind her he put on a dressing gown and, cursing the lack of slippers, went out into the corridor. Françoise was not in sight by the elevator; either it had already collected her or she was going down the stairs. Cautiously he took the staircase himself and then made for the first floor restaurant, trying to work out in his mind which of the windows gave the best view of the hotel forecourt.

Half a dozen eccentrics, English presumably, were having their coffee and rolls there instead of in their rooms. Near the entrance a girl was grimly counting cutlery. Venniker went across to the right-hand window. The man at the nearest table put down his paper to observe him.

At first he thought he was too late. Then he saw Françoise emerge from behind a column of the portico. She had presumably been signalling to the line of taxis that stood outside a larger hotel down the street. The front taxi had started towards her. It drew abreast of the portico and Françoise disappeared inside. He narrowed his eyes in an effort to make out the registration number. But the distance was too great. He was still trying when the taxi swung away in the direction of central Brussels.

Most of the people in the restaurant were watching him. He nodded, smiling politely towards the most interested table, man, wife and a small daughter. 'A friend leaving,' he said, in French.

Back upstairs, he went first to his grip and opened the lining. The two letters he had kept for Seagram were still there. It didn't look as though they had been moved although he couldn't now remember exactly how he had positioned them. If Françoise *had* searched the room before he returned the previous evening, that would have been the only interesting thing for her to find. On balance, he felt he had passed her tests, whatever they had amounted to.

As he threw the dressing gown on to the bed, some lingering trace of her presence entered his nostrils. Vaguely at first, then more strongly, he wished her back.

9

Notwithstanding the signs in the air the night before, it still hadn't rained. The alliance of leaden sky and stained glass made Seagram's expression unreadable as they stood together in the nave of the Cathedral. Holier persons kneeled and brooded silently in the gloom about them. Beyond the gigantic pulpit was a side chapel in which assorted Dukes of Brabant slept in marble shrouds.

Seagram said, 'I understand how you feel.'

Venniker peered at him, almost laughed. 'Do you? You know what it's like to be the axe that's used to murder somebody? You know what *that* feels like?'

He watched Seagram's shoulders lift and fall wearily.

'Let me tell you something. When I left England and came here I had the sensation of being released from a cage I'd been in most of my life. Being in prison for a crime I hadn't committed was the worst time of course. But even in London afterwards the cage was always there. I think of you as the person who did the most to free me from it. I've been poor most of the time since but I've been free. Last night when I stood looking at half a dead man I'd helped to kill hanging out of a hole in the wall I knew the cage was back.'

'That isn't true in any real sense – you were hardly more than a bystander.'

'It doesn't feel like that.'

Seagram thrust both hands deep in his pockets. He kicked the floor once or twice with the side of his shoe. 'So you don't feel you can give me any more help . . .'

'*More?*' Venniker shook his head in disbelief. 'What more do you need? All that's wanted now is to identify the taxi driver who picked up Françoise. This can be done by questioning the rank – it was a regular taxi stand. Why can't you do that yourself?'

'If I start making open inquiries in Brussels I must put my cards on the table with the Belgian police and I've no authority for that.'

'Isn't it about time you *asked* for it?'

Seagram said heavily, 'It's not that easy.' He looked away into the side chapel. 'Paul, you may not think I have any right to say this. You certainly don't owe me any favours for what happened in the past. I only did what I had to do and the fact that it helped you was incidental. But I have to ask you one more thing – as a personal favour if you like. I'm asking you not only because this case is important to me but also because I don't like ordinary people getting hurt as a result of a bunch of nuts or megalomaniacs deciding they're going to force their ideas down our throats. And I'll lay money that's exactly what will happen if we don't get Françoise and her group soon. Make the inquiry for me – find out the address she was taken to in the taxi.'

'But why *me* rather than getting the Belgian police in on the act?'

Seagram was hesitating. Eventually he said, 'There's something else affecting the attitude at the top in London towards bringing in the Belgians – that is, beyond admitting our interest in Jewkes, which is as far as we have gone so far. The agent said he believed that one of the leaders of the organization for which Jewkes worked *had important political British connections.*'

'You mean there's a politician working with Françoise?'

'Possibly – I don't know. I've given you the exact words the Americans passed on. People back home would like to have a better idea of what may be hatching under the stone before asking others to help roll it away.'

This time he laughed outright, so that some tourists rubber-necking beyond Seagram's shoulder looked back sharply. 'To hell with that! *Any minute* I could be on the spot with the Belgian police! How can I know that fingerprints won't be traced to me when they've gone over Ebner's apartment? I had a drink with him, I almost certainly touched the door and some of the furniture. You've got to tell them now to square *my* position.'

'I absolutely promise that if the Belgian police get a lead to you before we tell them the story, you'll be protected.'

He waved it away. 'There's another consideration we haven't mentioned yet. Ebner himself. We both know who Ebner was now.'

'We know who he might have been.'

'. . . who he *was*. It would be too much of a coincidence otherwise. Françoise said herself that he was an American Government agent who'd managed to get into a relationship with them. It fits exactly with the reports you've told me about. Which means that in addition to the Belgian police I'm going to have the U. S. Drugs Enforcement Agency, or whatever it calls itself, trying to catch up with me. Do you wonder I feel a distinct compulsion to take the next train out?'

Seagram had shifted so that his face was now caught by light that came through plain glass. He looked as though he drank too much these days. An amalgam of ambition and cynicism had hardened the mouth more than when Venniker had first met him. But there remained in the eyes that quality which above all else made him formidable. Honesty was Seagram's sword and sometimes his albatross.

He said, 'All right. I don't blame you.'

'What does that mean?'

'Forget what I've said. You've done your share. We'll find another way.' He put his hand out to shake on it. 'I mean that. And thank you for everything else.'

Venniker shook his head very slowly. 'May you rot,' he said.

'Why? I meant it.'

'I know. And that's the trouble with you.' He watched an old woman pass on the way to the altar with a candle. 'So . . . you want the girl identified. Then . . . finish?'

Seagram said, 'Yes, but . . .' then stopped. 'You want to do it?'

'I don't want to, but I will. After that it's back to Larche.'

'You'll try the taxi rank this morning?'

'Yes.'

They avoided looking at each other. Venniker walked across to the side chapel and read an inscription. Under that marble, Archduke Albert was laid out. He couldn't make out much more of the text. He knew he'd had a curious sort of escape. Saying no to Seagram would have amounted to something corruptive of his own spirit. There had been a trust between them to a degree he had known with no one else in his life. He still felt the sense of debt. But that wasn't the important thing. In the days and the weeks and the years ahead, he would need to know that Seagram hadn't found him wanting.

Seagram spoke behind him. 'She sounds an interesting case – Françoise. Exactly what drives her on, do you suppose? It's not crime obviously. Whereas with Moley Jewkes, whatever line he shoots to the world and to himself, it's just straight villainy. He wants money, and crime has always seemed the best way of getting it in sufficient quantities for life to be tolerable. But she doesn't fit into that scene at all. How can she accept it? Or is she much more cynical than I've understood?'

He went on without waiting for Venniker to answer. 'Did you enjoy sleeping with her?' He said it thoughtfully.

'Yes.'

'*Actively?*'

'Yes.'

'Although you knew she'd arranged Ebner's murder an hour or two before?'

'Yes.'

'Why?'

'Perhaps it was a plus factor. Perhaps I'm getting kinky.'

'You mean that?'

'Who knows?' He went back over his thoughts when he was lying beside her. He couldn't admit even to himself what his fears still were: that he was no longer capable of any sort of normal relationship.

Seagram said, 'I'm a policeman not a psychologist. As a policeman I just want to be sure she hasn't got into your bloodstream.'

If he told Seagram the truth, he'd have to say he wasn't at all certain himself. He shook his head. 'I'm still *your* agent. For the rest of today. After that I'll be a long way away.' He glanced at his watch. 'There's nothing else to talk about, is there?'

Seagram said, 'I'll have to go back to London again and report to the Commissioner. Let's check what we know to date. You've confirmed beyond doubt that the group Jewkes works for has explosives as well as being into drugs. And it doesn't mind killing when necessary. This girl, Françoise, is obviously one of the leaders of the group – perhaps *the* leader. She doesn't talk like a criminal and she's almost certainly a political nut of some sort. There's no clue at all to the identity of the other two people she spoke about and there's no hint of any British politician being involved – apart from the original information from the American source. Françoise is interested in using your place in France for storing stuff – unspecified – which doesn't become available in the Brussels area, according to her, but near Paris. She says she may be in touch with you about this?'

'Yes.'

'O.K. If you get a line on her you've got the number to telephone. Do your best, Paul.'

'I keep the money Françoise paid me . . . ?'

'A bonus.' Seagram looked towards the doors of the Cathedral. 'You go first.' He touched Venniker briefly on the elbow, a gesture made up of authority and gratitude. It was the second injunction of the day to look after himself, one from each camp. That must mean something.

Venniker stopped at a bar to look through the morning newspaper. Ebner's death was reported on an inside page. The explosion was described as mysterious; there were no other details except that the police were investigating. He felt a chill spreading under his rib cage. He wanted to be back in Larche, looking at the apricot trees, feeling the sun on his head, hearing the peacocks call across the grass.

Wandering through the Galeries Hubert while he summoned back his equilibrium he saw a lace blouse and bought it as a present for Opal. It was eleven thirty when he came out of the shop. He called a taxi at the end of the arcades and asked to be taken to the cab rank in the street outside his hotel.

Finding the driver who had picked up Françoise was the easiest thing of all. The man at the head of the rank looked at the fifty francs note in his hand but didn't take it at first. 'What do you want with the driver?'

'The girl he picked up had spent the night with me. I need to find her again. But she gave me no address.'

The man took the note with a shrug and went along the line.

At the fourth cab he looked back and raised a finger for Venniker to join him. It was as simple as that.

The driver remembered her without hesitation, but his report was discouraging. 'She gave no address. She just asked to be dropped in the Boulevard de Berlaymont.'

'You didn't see which way she went afterwards?'

'No. I noticed in my mirror that she stood and watched me drive away.'

Venniker cursed. 'Take me to the spot.'

It was a wasteland of glass and concrete boxes, a testimonial to man's inhumanity to space. Venniker looked about him. Above one of the boxes he could see the tower of the cathedral where he had been with Seagram earlier.

'Why would anyone come to this place?'

'Perhaps she works over there.' The driver pointed.

'Is it an office?'

The taxi driver stared, not quite believing that Venniker wasn't joking. 'You don't know Berlaymont?'

'No.'

'It's the office of the European Community – the home of the bureaucrats. They call it Berlaymort. A comfortable place to die, Berlaymort.'

Venniker caught Seagram with a broadcast call at Brussels airport a quarter of an hour before his London plane was due to leave. Seagram sounded apprehensive when he picked up the telephone. 'Who is this?'

'Paul Venniker. I had to talk to you before you took off.'

'Something wrong?'

'I thought your report to the Commissioner would be improved if it included the identity of Françoise.'

'*You've got it already?*'

'I had a little luck. That plus a helpful security guard who happens to be very observant when it comes to the way women look and dress. When Françoise left me she went to the Headquarters of the European Community, which I'm not very ashamed to admit I didn't recognize when it was shown to me. She didn't actually ask the taxi driver to take her to the building but to a street nearby.'

'Does she work for the Community?'

'No. But she's a close relative of someone who does work there and who is sufficiently important in This House, as the guard called it, for him and his colleagues to know her by sight because she visits now and then.'

Seagram said, 'We'll have to hurry, they've just broadcast the final call for my plane.'

'Françoise is Gail Landon. Her father is Sir Miles Landon who, they tell me, is one of the E.E.C. Commissioners. I remember him vaguely being a Minister in the Government back home before I left London. Presumably that's the connection with a politician the American source talked about. Now you know how the British contribution to the Common Market is working out.'

He enjoyed the silence at the other end. Seagram sounded suitably shaken when his voice came back. 'You're sure of this?'

'Absolutely.'

'The security guard at the E.E.C. building couldn't have confused your description with ...'

'The timing fitted exactly. She entered the Headquarters fifteen minutes after she left me at the hotel and went up to the thirteenth floor where her father has his office with the other Commissioners. She came out twenty minutes later. The guard noted the times in his register of visitors. He described the dress she was wearing – everything.'

'All right,' Seagram said, 'I buy it. You've saved a lot of trouble for everybody. You may have started a hell of a lot as well but that's not your worry. Tell me what you're going to do now.'

'I'm having a good meal at your expense and I'm catching the evening train to Paris. You know where to find me when you send my earnings.'

Seagram seemed to hesitate over his reply. Eventually he said in a resigned voice, 'All right.'

'Good luck with the Commissioner. I mean yours, not the E.E.C. one.' His morale was going up and up; already he felt free again. 'Offer him a peacock from me, special price.'

For lunch he went to the best restaurant he could find and afterwards spent a couple of hours in a cinema, the first time he had seen a film for years. He had hardly got back to his hotel room and begun to pack when the telephone rang. He knew then he had been a fool not to check out before lunch.

Seagram's relief at getting him was audible. 'Whatever it is,' Venniker said, 'the answer is no.'

Seagram said urgently, 'Paul, I've been trying to contact you for the past hour. I need you in London – as fast as you can get here.'

'You're joking.'

'Your story caused a hell of a stir when it hit the fan.'

'I can imagine. But . . .'

'Somebody very important wants to see you himself.'

'There's nothing to add to what I've told you. What would be the point?'

'He wants to hear it from you direct. Because of the implications.'

'Who are you talking about?'

Seagram sounded as though he was controlling himself with an effort. 'I can't go into this any more over the telephone. I know it's inconvenient. I'm asking you as a personal favour to do this. You can be on your way again tomorrow afternoon.'

'When I left London I said to myself I was never going back.'

'Four or five hours at the outside, Paul. Would that hurt?'

To the extent that a balance could ever be struck in these things, he'd discharged his debt to Seagram. He felt no more obligation. Yet he couldn't refuse the appeal in his voice. And there was something else; excitement and the sense of being the focus of events were at work giving him a charge that already was taking the sting out of Ebner's murder and his own part in that. Venniker half-cursed, half-sighed.

'All right, I'm a fool – but where do I come to and when?'

'Heathrow's no good. When my plane landed this afternoon they were just calling a strike – it's closed now and I suggest the overnight train ferry. When you get into Victoria, telephone my office at the Yard and we'll get a car down to pick you up.'

He tried telephoning Opal at Larche before he left. There was no reply. He was slightly surprised, but she might have gone to buy things in Mersac. There was no good reason to imagine anything wrong; and he could telephone her before the journey back from London tomorrow. When he was in his sleeper somewhere between Brussels and the Channel coast, he thought of her again. In the vaguest possible way he felt that something had changed.

10

In the empty street below the window of Seagram's office in Scotland Yard, a police patrol moved to and fro. More police were on watch in the side approaches. There were no cars parked anywhere in sight. 'The age of the bomber,' said Seagram. 'Cosy, isn't it?'

'How long have things been like this?' Venniker asked.

'Not all that amount of time, I suppose. There's been a slow build-up. It's a particularly bad period we've run into during the last few months.'

'What are you expecting today?'

'Some joker telephoned a newspaper an hour ago. He said he was about to blow up the Yard because his sister had been raped by a policeman. The idea of blowing things up as a protest is so fashionable these days that you can't ignore any warning. He described the type and amount of explosive he was going to use and it made sense technically. So what can you do except take it seriously?'

'Françoise's group is the worst of your headaches at the moment, is it – even though they haven't killed anybody . . .?'

'. . . yet,' said Seagram. A constable came in with two mugs of tea. 'The trouble is we still know so little about them. What are they – Anarchists, Revolutionary Communists, Alternative Society nuts? We have no idea, not a clue. These small groups come and go. One day Françoise and her lot will either get tired or caught. Then we wait for the next one.'

'Is it getting worse?'

'This sort of thing will die down eventually – like everything else. But it's going to be uncomfortable until it does.'

Seagram sighed. 'Meanwhile we have to try and work out the scenario Françoise is playing to.'

'What do *you* think it is?'

'I can only make a guess. Stage one – get publicity with

bangs and excitement, warnings to the newspapers. Stage two – create fear in the public, loss of confidence, a growing feeling that neither the police nor anyone else in authority can give adequate protection. Then – hope for a slight change of mood, people beginning to be grateful that *they* haven't been targets so far, that it's always somebody else's property, and rich men's property at that. A little admiration creeps in. So that you're ready for the next phase.'

'Killing?'

'Probably. But don't ask me who. Policemen perhaps. Special Branch could name you a lot of people who would say killing coppers is good. Of course it gets dressed up with fancy phrases like the Long March through the Institutions. But behind it all there's something personal, some bitterness or frustration being worked out. These jokers are like the child who pushes down the house of bricks its father has built because that's the most effective way of hiding its own inability to do as well.' Seagram spat a tea leaf against the window pane, then picked it off. 'Do your own thing, man, and if it means cutting up your neighbour, well, that's *too* bad.'

The telephone on his desk rang. Venniker watched Seagram as he picked the receiver up and listened. He wore a blue pinstripe suit and what was probably a sports club tie. He was smarter, more at ease, here in his own environment. But the air of somebody on his way up and wanting to look the part had faded. His shirt was crumpled and the shoulders of his jacket had not been brushed for days.

Seagram replaced the receiver. 'We're on. Home Office in fifteen minutes. The Commissioner says he'll be late so we're going in to the Home Secretary without him. I suggest we walk – it's hardly worth getting my car.'

The youth who received them in an ante-chamber had long curly hair and coat lapels that touched his armpits. In due course he ushered them through another door. 'Home Secretary,' he said, 'this is Chief Superintendent Seagram, with Mr Venniker.'

The room was vast, the man rising from behind a desk tiny. A neat urban pixie: in his reading light the half-moon glasses straddling his nose momentarily shone like dipped headlights.

Then he whipped them off with a large flourish. 'Splendid! *Splendid!*' He was kicking himself into animation like a man starting a motor cycle. 'Come and sit *comfortably*.' He pointed with the spectacles towards a leather settee and armchairs arranged round a low table.

'I have heard an account of your adventures Mr Venniker – very interesting. You seem to have gone about your task with great skill. No doubt the Chief Superintendent here has conveyed our appreciation.'

The Home Secretary paused fractionally. 'Of course, what you say amounts to a very serious allegation. As regards the girl you have identified as Françoise.'

'I suppose so.'

'I don't think I've ever met Miss Landon myself but her father is an old political colleague of mine – a man of great integrity. I should not wish him to be upset by being told of this if there were any possibility of a mistake. What I should like to hear from you first is why you are certain you identified her correctly.'

'I described her to the security guard at the E.E.C. building, her clothing and . . .'

'You mean her dress is in some way unique?' He was being not quite sardonic.

'No, but her whole appearance is fairly distinctive. She's a very attractive woman. What it amounts to is that Gail Landon fits my description and entered the building at the right time.'

'But you and the security guard never saw her together so that you could confirm you were each referring to the same person.'

'No.'

The Home Secretary turned to Seagram. 'This is the one factor linking Miss Landon with the Brussels group . . .'

'Naturally we shall be investigating further to get corroboration, sir.'

'Yes indeed.' The Home Secretary produced a smile like a gun that demanded instant and total co-operation. 'I should hope so.'

'There is of course the matter of her past record, sir,' Seagram opened a file he had brought with him.

'What does that amount to?'

'A conviction for obstructing the police as a picket during an industrial dispute. Nothing else of a *criminal* nature. But she was quite prominent in agitation at her university: sit-ins, organizing marches of protest, raising funds for trade unionists during a strike.'

'I see,' said the Home Secretary. 'How very sinister. I hope, Chief Superintendent, you are not holding it too much against me that I sold flags for the Republicans at the time of the Spanish Civil War.'

'No, sir.'

'Good. *Very* good.' On the Home Secretary's lap his fingers were working against each other as though rubbing invisible tobacco. 'She is not known to belong to any group favouring organized violence, I take it.'

'No, sir.'

'Very well.' He sat back; the menacing smile reappeared. 'You come from Bedgley, Venniker, I understand?'

'Originally.'

'A part of my constituency. Sound folk in Bedgley. Are your family still there?'

'I have no relatives alive.'

'But is that a good reason for going off to live in France? No Bedgley black pudding in France.' He was being jolly while he made his mind up about something. 'Think what you're missing.'

Venniker began, 'If that's all you needed from me, I'll ...'

Seagram said quickly, 'I think Mr Venniker hopes to get an early ferry back. As you know, flights out of London Airport are grounded.'

The Home Secretary raised his eyebrows. 'I see. Well, Mr Venniker, you have heard the Chief Superintendent say that he will be pressing on with his investigation. I hope we can rely on your continued co-operation in this very delicate and important matter.'

When Venniker didn't reply he went on, 'I understand there's a good chance of the girl making contact with you again. Presumably you'll keep the Chief Superintendent informed of everything.' He produced his pistol smile. 'More than most people you must feel you have first-hand experience of the evil of one aspect of this group's activities.'

Venniker frowned. 'I don't ...'

'I believe your friend Miss Rayner was a heroin addict when you found her in Rome.'

Seagram's gaze stayed on the cover of his file. Venniker felt the blood rising in his neck. It had simply not occurred to him that Seagram would make inquiries about Opal. Yet it was obvious now he thought about it – a necessary part of the security planning for the Brussels operation. And there was no good reason why he himself should resent the fact that this gnome-like creature with a perpetual air of sardonic scepticism had been told. But he did resent it. Because Opal was a part of his life that was nothing to do with anyone else.

'Nobody is forced to take drugs,' he heard himself say. 'If people want to go to hell they'll find a way even if you eliminate every pusher in the world and destroy every poppy seed.'

'And you're quite indifferent to the morality of the pushers?'

'Their morality doesn't interest me. I just don't like them and I don't like drugs. Put me down as basically anti but not very zealous.'

'I see.' The Home Secretary looked slyly at Seagram. 'Well, I clearly mustn't try to force you to be zealous, Mr Venniker.'

The door to the anteroom opened and the youth who had received Venniker and Seagram reappeared. The knot of his tie was as large as his chin. His appearance seemed remarkably modish for the Whitehall Venniker had expected to find; he also looked very clever. Bending over the back of the Home Secretary's chair, he said without too much unction, 'The Commissioner has arrived, sir, with the Permanent Secretary. Mr Fox is also here.'

'Fox? Where does he come from?'

The youth bent closer, whispered. 'Ah yes,' said the Home Secretary. 'One of those. Well we might as well have them all in.'

Once more the youth whispered soft advice. 'Yes,' said the Home Secretary. 'But since Mr Venniker is so intimately involved in all this I would like him to stay.' He was enjoying himself, the fingers still working, the eyes on Seagram. 'He may indeed have something to contribute.'

The clever youth's eyes also rested on Seagram for a moment, waiting to see if a rash leap to remedy the situation might come from that quarter. Getting no support, he retired in silence through the door. A full minute passed before it opened again and the youth led in a trio to sit in the remaining armchairs. The Home Secretary greeted each with a nod and then said briskly, 'Now we're all assembled, I'd like to consider the situation that presents itself in the light of the facts uncovered by the Metropolitan Police. Or perhaps I should say, by Mr Venniker here.' Fitting a cigarette into a holder, he paused to watch their expressions as they viewed Venniker, then sat back, looking towards the Permanent Secretary. 'Would you care to start, Denis?'

The Permanent Secretary was gaunt and unlovely with a bony white scalp; a chain hung from a waistcoat button hole with a silver pencil at the end of it. Swinging the pencil he said, with his eyes apparently shut, 'As I understand it, Home Secretary, we now strongly suspect that one of the ringleaders in this Brussels conspiracy is Gail Landon who is Sir Miles Landon's daughter. According to your personal recollection ...'

The Home Secretary shook his head, 'My wife's, Denis, far more reliable.'

'... according to your wife's recollection, she's been estranged from her father in the past and although that's over she's not actually living with him in Brussels. She sometimes joins him, however, on his trips to this country which he makes regularly ...'

'... in order to keep himself abreast with affairs and to ensure his political reputation at home is burnished against the day when Brussels no longer holds charms,' said the Home Secretary. He singled out Venniker for a smile as though they were secret allies.

The Permanent Secretary opened his eyes and rested them impassively on the clever youth who had seated himself a little apart with paper and pen. 'Much is known to you, Home Secretary, which is denied to mere officials.'

The Home Secretary allowed his smile to broaden a fraction. He gave the Permanent Secretary a married nod. 'Go on, Denis.'

'These visits, we can guess, solve the problem of how the drugs – and probably the explosives too – have been getting in so regularly without a whisper from any of the usual sources which report to the police. The girl is making use of her father's status to bring them over. The baggage of a Commissioner of the European Economic Community must provide admirable security. The girl simply adds her suitcases to it. Of course she is then faced with the task of distributing the stuff to her associates and the criminal outlets they've established. No doubt the police will arrange to have her followed when she comes here next.'

The Metropolitan Police Commissioner, whose first cue this was, had taken the seat next to Seagram. He had his arms folded and his body twisted slightly away from the others as though to register disapproval either of Venniker's presence or of the meeting or both. 'Of course, we shall be on her heels as soon as she appears next time. But I really must take the Belgian Sûreté into our confidence now. They've so far been told nothing of what's going on, they've simply been made aware of our interest in the man Jewkes, alias Arundel. With the murder of this undercover American agent and the evidence produced by Venniker of the Landon girl's apparent complicity, we have to . . .'

'Of course,' said the Home Secretary with great emphasis. He pointed with the cigarette holder to show how much he agreed. 'You're quite right. However, for the moment I would prefer you to – to pause. No more than that. There are considerations I must pay attention to. In the present state of relations between the Government and the rest of the European Community, for it to get about that drugs and perhaps worse are being smuggled in the baggage of a British Commissioner over there could have a slightly . . . unhinging effect. I also must discuss with the Foreign Secretary how Landon himself is to be told of the suspicions affecting his daughter. He might feel obliged to resign and that could also be an embarrassment at this particular moment.'

A vein was signalling in the Commissioner's neck. He opened his mouth but the Home Secretary had already started again.

'Don't think I'm interfering, Commissioner. I accept that the Sûreté must be told as soon as possible. But I should be glad if you would wait until you have word from me.' He directed his smile towards the Commissioner and Seagram for a good four seconds. 'Meanwhile I know there's plenty for your chaps to be getting on with.'

'Of course one isn't yet clear how big an organization one is up against,' somebody said. It was Fox. He had been silent until then. 'One just doesn't know,' he repeated.

'But you have views,' said the Home Secretary. His expression became disarmingly attentive.

Fox gave a preparatory cough. He was the most immaculate figure present if not as modish as the youth. Flowering from his breast pocket, not too ostentatiously, was a handkerchief that exactly matched his damson silk tie. He might have been a Gentile merchant banker, or a fugitive from an advertising agency. 'It's not easy to go into details in these circumstances' – he glanced significantly at Venniker – 'but the question that has to be asked is – is HANGMAN *just* another private-enterprise group of the kind we've seen before?'

'Why shouldn't it be?' asked the Commissioner brusquely.

'First the use of drugs as a weapon. It's very odd. And how did they manage to undercut the other drugs suppliers?'

'Presumably they bought well in the first place,' said the Permanent Secretary, swinging his silver pencil rhythmically. 'Or they could have a very rich member in the gang. Even anarchists are liable to inherit fortunes now and then.'

'Gail Landon,' said Fox ignoring all interventions, 'was of course quite extreme at university.'

'True,' said the Home Secretary, without even glancing at Seagram. 'So where does that lead you?'

'This is a well-planned guerrilla war.' Fox looked with slightly dilated eyes at each person in turn as he spoke, omitting only Venniker and the clever youth. 'The areas where the drugs have been peddled are where a good many of the present and future servants of the Constitution are – in the Services, the universities, certain schools. The buildings being blown up are for the most part houses of what is thought of as the Establishment. HANGMAN isn't the first group to choose these targets. But doesn't its efficiency and resources suggest that behind people like this girl Françoise, there is something else – manipulating them, funding them, *directing their attack?*'

The Commissioner had begun to tap his fingers on the arm of his chair. There was a brief silence. 'Yes,' said the Home Secretary, 'I see. And the evidence to support this theory ...'

'None. But I recommend we look very carefully indeed.'

'Of course.' The Home Secretary's eyes swivelled. 'Commissioner?'

'We shall naturally keep an open mind, Home Secretary,' said the Commissioner heavily, 'as always. Anything in the way of *fact* that Mr Fox can contribute will be much appreciated. I must add this, however. Given the availability in our society of explosives to practically any nut who wants them, you only need three or four like-minded nuts, with some cash and a knowledge of the drugs world and a determination to leave their mark on us all, for something like HANGMAN to emerge. Nothing more.'

'Quite so,' said the Home Secretary. He had enjoyed himself. 'We must be prepared for anything of course. Eh, Mr Venniker?' It was his final insult to the others. 'Well, I think we're all agreed ...' He consulted his watch. The audience was over.

In the anteroom they split up without farewells, the clever youth hovering about them with an enigmatic smile. Fox lingered a while over removing his bowler hat and umbrella from their peg, one eye on Venniker. Eventually he disappeared through the door. His voice came faintly back from the corridor, calling to the Permanent Secretary ahead of him.

'Come and look at St. James' Park,' said Seagram to Venniker. 'I feel like some air.'

They took the short cut through Downing Street, down the steps and across Horse Guards Parade. The sun was out and a southerly breeze danced on the surface of the lake. Ducks cruised in and out of weeping willow branches. They sat on a bench and appraised the girls in their summer dresses.

'You'll have a bite of lunch with me,' Seagram said.

'Thank you. I'd like to get away soon afterwards if you don't mind.'

'No urge to look round?'

'None.'

'Don't you want to see your old haunts?'

'London's just a piece of the past for me. Nothing more. I don't want to dig it up. Tell me, who or what is Fox?'

Seagram laughed shortly. 'Fox is a funny. You can't have a meeting about bombs or terrorists without a funny turning up. They'll add two and two and make eight for you.'

'Sometimes it may do, I suppose.'

'Sometimes, not often.'

'You don't believe there's something else behind Françoise – the I.R.A. for example?'

'I don't have a view. What I *do* know is that Fox's ideas are too bloody fashionable. The result is that they're catching on with ordinary villains. Every bank robber who gets caught now says to himself – perhaps there's a way out if I claim I did it for political reasons. Who shall I choose – the I.R.A., the Palestinians, the Cornish Freedom Fighters? The only answer to that is – maybe you did it for any or all of them, *but you also did it for yourself son, because you wanted to do it.* If we give way on that we might as well give up altogether.'

'Fox kept mentioning HANGMAN – everybody at that meeting seemed to have heard of it before except me. Is HANGMAN what the group in Brussels call themselves?'

Seagram grimaced. 'I'm sorry – I thought I'd told you when we met in Mersac. Before, or immediately after, every explosion there's been a telephone message to a newspaper. The caller says he's speaking for HANGMAN and gives a code number. Yes, it's what Françoise and those others call themselves – HANGMAN.'

Venniker looked across the park at the Whitehall skyline. The buildings seemed cleaner than when he had seen them last; but perhaps it was just the effect of the summer. 'HANGMAN is an odd name to choose. I'd have expected something more – more evocative, more *political.* Why HANGMAN?'

'God knows. It's only a bit more unlikely than The Angry Brigade. Do you remember *that?*

'Can you imagine anyone actually choosing the name *Angry Brigade?* But somebody did. There's probably no rational reason behind it. Somebody somewhere giggled and said, "What about HANGMAN?" And that was that.' Seagram stood up. 'Let's go. I'll take you to a place on the river for lunch.'

They sat over steaks and draught bitter in a Wapping pub. There were pink-shaded wall lights and prints of Olde London in frames which had strips of velvet on them. Outside the gutters were lined with Mercs and Jags. Somebody nearby was quoting the price f.o.b. Amsterdam.

'So this is Wapping,' Venniker said. 'You could certainly have fooled me.'

'It's changed. Here and there.'

'Are you paying for this lunch personally?'

'Yes.'

He smiled. 'Thank you.'

'Do you suppose anybody else here is doing the same?'

'Probably not.'

'So who really pays for *them*?'

'Come back tomorrow or the next day. Perhaps we shall all find out soon.'

Venniker looked through the windows on to the empty river. 'Tell me what you make of things now. I don't mean the case. Everything here. What do you think of it all?'

Seagram reached for his beer. 'London reminds me of the Shakespeare play in the examination I took the year before I left school and became a police cadet. I remember only one thing from *Julius Caesar*, apart from Mark Anthony's speech. The Ides of March.'

'Are the dead walking the street yet?'

'No. But there are other signs. Fortune tellers howl, women copulate with bears. The people listen and wait. While they're waiting, they have their diversions of course – drink, drugs, fantasy sex. And violence.'

'If you're as pessimistic about the future as that, I wonder you can bother with little problems like HANGMAN.'

'I didn't say *I* was pessimistic. Others may be. I don't think my view of the future has changed a lot in thirty years. I don't worry that much, as long as there's something that's got to be done that doesn't seem hopelessly impossible. Killing

HANGMAN looks entirely possible to me. I'll get on with that and let the others bother about the future.'

When coffee came he said, looking into his cup, 'I'm sorry the Home Secretary brought up Opal Rayner this morning. I didn't realize that particular file had been passed to him.'

Venniker shrugged.

'You understand I couldn't avoid making inquiries myself?'

'It doesn't matter.'

'How is she?'

'She believes she's cured. I think there's a good chance.'

'I meant – have you been in touch in the last few days?'

That sensation of a change, something different, came back. Venniker stared at Seagram, wondering if there could be a hidden meaning to the question. But his expression was normal. 'I've spoken to her once on the telephone – she seemed all right. I'll be calling her when I get ashore in France to tell her I'm on my way back.'

'What about the future – will you stay together?'

He raised his eyebrows, watching the white-coated boy behind the bar as he poured double Curaçaos for the next table. Sitting here, he could think about it as dispassionately as he observed the liqueur rising in the glasses. 'I don't know. There are other things she ought to do. I wouldn't try to stop her. She's young.'

As they walked back to Seagram's car, Venniker said, 'That's all then.'

'You'll telephone me if Françoise contacts you.'

'Yes.'

'My driver can take you on to Victoria after he's dropped me at the Yard.' They drove in silence for a while. Seagram looked at dandruff on the sleeve of his jacket and brushed at it with his hand. 'I hope you're not too sorry I looked you up.'

'I didn't enjoy being involved in killing Ebner.'

'It wasn't your responsibility.'

'That's what Françoise said. It doesn't make it seem better.'

'Did you sleep with her *in spite* of what happened – or because of it?'

He looked Seagram in the eyes, and shrugged. He didn't know what to say. He glanced at his watch. 'Two thirty. I shan't be across the Channel before this evening. That means I'll have to catch the morning train to Cahors from Paris.'

When the car dropped Seagram at the Yard, Venniker leaned through the window. 'My bank is the Credit Agricole in Mersac. They'll be happy to hear from you.'

'I'll talk to Finance tomorrow.'

They smiled at each other. 'Thank you again,' said Seagram.

'I'm glad if I helped you.'

'You know you did that.'

'Come again one day. But after you've retired. I could do with some assistance about the place.'

'I might take you up on that.' Seagram held up a hand. 'Safe journey.' He went briskly through the glass doors.

Near Victoria station an ambulance passed the car, its bell ringing, Venniker noticed the driver stiffen in his seat. But when they got round the next corner and saw the cause, a cyclist knocked off his machine, he relaxed again.

'Any bombs today?' Venniker asked him.

'Not that I've heard,' the driver said. 'Nice and quiet today.'

11

There was not the smallest breath of breeze. Heat had settled on the *causse* like an animal, snuffing even the scent of the lavender. As Venniker drove down the track to Larche, he saw, in the shadowed refuge behind the barn, a rich man's car at rest. He noted it was a Rolls Royce Camargue. A first, he thought: tourists in search of the elusive Château Larche had driven up in Mercedes, in Lamborghinis and Maseratis, once even in a pre-war Alfa. But this was the first Camargue. Entranced at their new-found comfort, the hens moved in and out of the velvet darkness beneath its wheels.

He reversed the 2CV, parked it alongside and stood back to admire the effect. One of the peacocks approached him. It rooted in the dust at his feet. He was certain it was really acknowledging his return. It felt good to be back.

Walking down the path to the gatehouse, he was suddenly not so sure. A figure, apparently naked, sat on one of the benches under the chestnut tree. It was a man, youngish in build, with hair tied in a ponytail. Something about the face, even at this distance, was familiar. The man lay back with eyes closed, his arms dangling behind him, a wine bottle and some dishes on the table beside him.

As Venniker hesitated between crossing over to him and going straight to the gatehouse, Opal appeared in the doorway. She was carrying a bottle of Volvic in one hand, a transistor radio in the other. He waved.

She ran towards him and they kissed. She tasted of peaches and the white wine he had bought last week, her mouth warm and soft this time, as he remembered it in Rome.

'Did it go well?'

'More or less.'

'Lots of loot?'

'Five thousand Swiss francs so far. More on the way.'

'Super!'

'I tried telephoning you twice. There was no reply.'

She made a face. 'I must have been out. I wondered why I hadn't heard from you after the first call.'

He looked at her, holding her away from him. She seemed transformed, there was no other word for the change in the few days he had been away. Her skin had tanned and come alive again. In the bikini top she was wearing even her breasts seemed fuller. He put his hand under one of them. 'You're *fat*!'

'I can't stop eating.'

Venniker glanced towards the benches under the chestnut tree. The man had opened his eyes and was inspecting them, one hand now supporting his neck. 'Is this Teas for Tourists?'

Opal giggled. 'Come and meet him.'

'Who is it?'

'Don't you recognize him?'

'No.'

'It's Jay Daye.'

Jay Daye. Of course, he told himself, that face, that hair; Jay Daye for Our Day, hadn't that been the publicity tag? Jay Daye in Person – the glitter suit and the platform soles, the microphone held to the shouting mouth, and all around the nymphets surging in paroxysms, wetting their pants. Our Day, they sang; Jay, they screamed. J A Y! But that was years ago, even before he had left England, had left that cardboard and tinsel world to others.

'How did he get here? Does he know you?'

Opal had taken his hand to lead him over. 'He remembered me from one of Marisa's parties in Rome two years ago. He was there on a visit.'

'Jesus,' he said. 'A spot of main-lining with him would really set you up now, wouldn't it?'

'Don't get tense – he's not on the needle. He never has been – he told me. They were just out to nail him, the police. It was a put-up job.'

He drew breath, hardly able to believe she was serious; but they had almost reached the chestnut tree. He nodded at Daye. 'Paul Venniker.'

In the flesh, he was smaller – the way they always turned out – than the image created by the camera, by those magazine action photographs, always angled upwards from somewhere below the knee-caps. The plucked eyebrows and the white make-up had gone but he still wore his other trade marks, the rubies in the lobes of each ear. The eyes were the palest possible blue, as evilly innocent as ever.

'You must be bushed, driving in this heat,' Daye said. He was not, after all, naked; he was wearing a pair of saffron-coloured briefs and sandals. On the grass beside him were a Ted Lapidus shirt with triangular pearl buttons and a pair of trousers.

'Did you go all the way to Brussels and back in that crate?'

'No. I parked it in Cahors and did the journey by train.' He wondered what Opal had said about his trip.

'I go for this place.' Daye extended his hand along the line of oak trees. 'Great.'

'What brings you to these parts?'

Daye stretched out his hand again, this time towards Opal. When she smiled, he shrugged at Venniker with his eyes half-closed. He was at ease to a degree that just fell short of insolence. 'I was driving through Mersac on my way south, my place is in Cap Ferrat. I stopped for a meal and there was Opal trying to tie two *baguettes* on the back of a Honda with some insulating tape. Fantastic.'

Venniker sat down on the other bench. 'I see.'

'Have you eaten?' Opal asked.

'Not lately.'

'There's some chicken we bought in Mersac. I'll make a salad and bring it out.' She turned rather quickly and went off to the gatehouse; grass clung to the backs of her legs. The peacocks were moving down from the barn to intercept her in case there was anything worth having in the dishes she was carrying into the kitchen.

'She looks terrific,' Daye said.

'You met in Rome, I gather?'

Daye smiled. 'She tells me she's off the needle.'

'She's trying.' He sat back and smelled the sweat from Daye's armpits. 'I particularly don't want anybody to spoil that.'

'Meaning me?'

'Perhaps.'

'You think I shoot?'

'Shouldn't I?'

'Because of what you remember reading in the press . . .?'

He hesitated. Daye said, 'You're wrong, man. You just bought what *they* said. I tried it when I was nineteen. I'd stopped even before I had my first hit record. And I never tried it again. But the fuzz didn't care about that. Jay Daye sings druggy songs so we'll bust him for drugging. I *had* to be shooting. That's what the system said. So they planted some on me. End of story.'

Daye reached for the Volvic Opal had brought and poured some into a wine glass. 'People didn't know that. They believed what they were told. But the fuzz knew the truth and so did the judge. And so did I.' He smiled. 'We belong to the same club, Paul. Busted for something we didn't do . . .'

When Venniker stared, he stretched out a hand and placed it on his forearm – the fingers stroked and then squeezed gently, trying for a reaction, the pale blue eyes all the time on Venniker's face.

'Opal told me. Not all the details, but that you'd been in a police frame once, up in Bedgley. Congratulations.'

Venniker felt irritation twitching the muscles of his face. All right! He *had* been framed by a copper in Bedgley who cared nothing about the truth, only about getting to the top of the pile where the pickings would be sweetest. But he didn't want to be a partner with Daye, not in any way, not even just swapping stories about bent policemen.

'What did they plant on *you*?' Daye asked.

'It doesn't matter now.'

'A gun?'

'It was a cosh.'

'And you waited outside while the other two went into the house and killed the old man.'

'They simply told me they were borrowing money from him. I sat in the car outside. I was a fool perhaps. But that was all.'

'Too bad,' said Daye. He smiled: suddenly Venniker knew he didn't believe him. Like every other man to whom he told the story. Except Seagram.

'How close are you and Opal?' Daye asked.

'We get along.' He wondered what Opal had said on the subject.

'No strings?'

'No strings.'

'She tells me she's a fabric designer. Is she good?'

'Yes.'

'She's not planning to do it here.' It was a statement, not a question.

'She'll move on when she's ready. London's probably where she ought to be. There's no hurry.'

'There *are* other places of course,' Daye said. 'Apart from London, I mean.' An insect was crawling across the table towards some crumbs. He picked up his glass and poured water on it and watched it wriggle. 'I might be able to help. You wouldn't mind that?'

'I wouldn't mind.'

Opal was walking towards them carrying a tray. She placed it in front of Venniker and sat down beside him. 'What were you saying?'

Venniker reached for a lettuce heart. 'I said you were a good designer.'

She smiled across at Daye. Venniker watched Opal pouring wine into his glass. Something had been said on the subject before he arrived, he was sure.

'What took you to Brussels?' asked Daye.

'I had some paintings I thought I might be able to sell. I didn't sell them but something else came up so it wasn't a wasted trip.' He sliced himself a piece of Pont L'Evêque. 'What do *you* do since you gave up show business?'

'Nothing special. My home's in France now. I have some property here and in Italy that takes up some time. I keep in touch with what's new. Mostly I just relax.' He stretched and yawned but there was something a shade studied about the movements. He conveyed controlled energy, even purpose, not relaxation.

Daye reluctantly reached down beside the bench for the shirt and slacks and drew them on. 'I've got to go. I said I'd be back in the Cap this morning.'

They walked up the gravel path to the barn. Daye rubbed a knuckle against Opal's cheek. 'Good-bye baby.' She smiled. 'Good-bye Jay.'

Daye climbed into the Camargue. From the carpet beside his feet he took a pair of wrap-round shades and fitted them to his face. When he settled back with his hands on the steering wheel, he became remote as though behind a plate glass wall.

The Camargue slid up the track towards the orchard, riding the bumps as though they were marshmallow. In the lee of the barn the hens crouched motionless, bemused by the removal of their palace. Venniker glanced at Opal. She had torn a leaf from a bush and was breaking it up.

Back at the table under the chestnut he sliced more of the Pont L'Evêque. 'Did Aldo turn up regularly?'

'He took yesterday off and today. His mother's ill.'

She ran a hand through her hair; the sun had made it much paler than before he went away, it was almost platinum. 'He says the apricots should be good.'

He noticed a stagnant pool of water below the kitchen window.

'So you made out all right,' he said.

'I told you I would.'

He drank more wine, and half-closed his eyes against the sun.

'I see the kitchen drain's blocked up.'

She followed his eyes. 'It's probably grease.'

She turned her head towards the barn. 'Fantastic car.'

'Fantastic.'

'He keeps a Lamborghini as a run-around at Cap Ferrat.'

'Great,' he said. There was a copy of yesterday's *Figaro* beside him on the bench and he picked it up. 'I've never known you buy a newspaper.'

'I didn't. Jay brought it.'

He scanned the headlines and threw it down; then picked it up again. The story in the right-hand column, date-lined Brussels, was about Ebner. The Belgian police had announced the result of inquiries into his background. His true name was apparently de Maggio. He had been to the University of Dallas where he had been a prominent figure in student unrest. After leaving the University he had joined the Weathermen faction of the Students for a Democratic Society group and gone underground. He had been the only one who had evaded arrest when the F.B.I. caught up with a Weathermen unit after a series of bombings in New York. There was still no information about those responsible for his murder. Perhaps, said a police spokesman, it was a result of a feud between rival revolutionary groups. In Washington the F.B.I. had declined all comment.

'What's so interesting?' asked Opal.

He put the paper down and felt his heart thudding. 'Somebody dead. Nobody you know.' He watched an aeroplane cross the sky. 'You picked him up, didn't you – Daye?'

She laughed in derision. 'No! It was just as he told you – I'd bought some bread when he called out from the car.'

He told himself he had to believe her.

He decided to have a shower in the dry-stone hut he had converted into a combined bathroom and lavatory when he first moved to the gatehouse. By the time he had put on a change of clothing he felt more relaxed. Going back to the house he found Opal in the bedroom picking at a thread in a pair of jeans. She had the record player on very quietly. He gave her the lace blouse. He guessed she was wondering if he would want to make love to her.

He went to the window and stared at the *donjon* across the valley. He knew what he would say to her, in a world where one said exactly what one felt. *I don't want to make love to you. Not because I think it might be the fiasco it was before I went away. I have other reasons. I don't want to start again with you. Because it might get difficult to persuade myself you ought to make the break. If ever you are going to swim alone, maybe it ought to be soon. I've got to get used to that.*

He turned back to Opal, thinking he might even get some of it out, then paused, his eye caught by something white on the rug beside the bed. He picked it up, a triangular pearl button. He held it up. The time that had elapsed since he had seen the button's brothers on a Ted Lapidus shirt was approximately seventy-five minutes. He shook his head slowly. 'You slept with him.'

She stopped picking at the thread. Her face was tense. 'I was going to tell you.'

'You're a cow,' he said.

'Paul...'

'Just a cow.'

'Paul, listen...'

He struck her face with the back of his hand as hard as he could. 'No, listen to me.' Underneath his anger he could feel the relief that this was going to save him from saying the more difficult things he had thought of a moment ago. 'When you came here you were so damn near the end of the line I wasn't even sure you'd survive six months. Somehow you did. By the second time you came back from the clinic I really hoped you'd got the message and were beginning to grow up. But, I was wrong, wasn't I? You'll never learn to say no.'

Opal lay across the bed, a little blood oozing from the corner of her mouth. He felt sick with self-hatred. Eventually she said, 'I'm glad you did that. Because it's made me accept what I'd refused to face up to before.' She wiped the corner of her mouth with her fingers and looked at them with mild interest. She was very composed. 'You're right – I was almost finished in Rome. But you got me standing up again. Without your help I could never have kicked heroin. I admit it. The trouble is that in helping me you made me think I mattered as a person.'

He was aware of a chill inside him.

'What I've been instead is a sort of atonement. Through me you were paying off your conscience over the girl in Shepherd Market, who died according to you because you didn't take the trouble to be more caring, more *involved*.' She tried to mimic him saying the word but her lip had begun to swell. 'You're kind, Paul, – dumb animals are always going to get a break from you. But *feeling* – what about feeling? Once you'd got rid of your bloody sense of guilt, there wasn't any feeling left, was there?'

For her, it was a long speech. He sneered. 'Where did you learn your psychiatry – off matchboxes?'

She ignored his words. 'Once I was getting well, really well, there was no chance of a relationship. Which is slightly sad because I'd begun to love you. I *know* there wasn't anything I wanted more than to stay with you and *matter* to you. But we could never have got on to that wavelength. Because I've never existed for you in my own right.'

'Whereas with Jay Daye . . .' he said.

'I would never expect anything of a relationship with Jay. In any case he's not particularly interested in women these days. He prefers boys.'

'He must have been quite a challenge for you.'

She said nothing.

'You *did* sleep with him?'

'Yes.'

'I'm interested in exactly why.'

'You wouldn't understand. It doesn't matter now, anyway.'

'Tell me.'

She drew breath deep into her lungs. 'It may sound childish. But I wanted to find out if anybody else . . . could desire me. You didn't. I wondered if the trouble was really me.'

'You're unbelievable,' he said. But his anger had drained away leaving just bitterness.

Opal said, 'I'd like to leave tomorrow.'

'And then?'

'I told Jay about my designing. He said if I go and stay in his villa at Cap Ferrat he'll introduce me to somebody in the business who owes him a favour.'

'Where is this somebody?'

'Nice, I believe.'

He couldn't stop himself saying it. 'Handy for the clinic anyway.'

When she didn't rise to the insult, he went on, 'Do you honestly think you'll be in any sort of shape for designing – for *anything* – after a few weeks with Daye and the crowd he must have round him?'

She said patiently, 'He's not on drugs – I'm sure of that, it's something you can tell. But even if he were I can handle myself. He wouldn't have any chance of starting me off again.'

'Quite apart from the drugs angle – and I'm not denying he *could* have been framed by the police – Daye's name stank in London. I never met him in those days but I heard enough.'

'About what?'

'He's got some twist, some kink.' He frowned, trying to remember.

'He may have. But that's his affair.' She wasn't making sense;

the really deadly thing was the fact that she thought Daye was worth defending.

'When exactly did he turn up?' Venniker asked.

'Two days ago. He gave me dinner. He spent the first night at the hotel. Last night he stayed here. I asked him to.'

'Thank you,' he said. He went out to look at the lavender and the fruit trees. The smells he had looked forward to for almost a week were all there but they meant nothing now.

Later in the evening she made a meal. He ate a little and steadily drank the bottle of whisky he had bought on the ferry crossing from England. When she was washing dishes at the sink Opal said, 'I would like to know how you are sometimes. May I write?'

'It's up to you.' He couldn't wait for her to go.

The next day he drove her to Cahors. She carried everything she owned in the soft-top suitcase with which she had arrived twelve months before. His mood had changed again; now he could think of only two things – her vulnerability and his own hypocrisy over her night with Daye. On the platform as the train drew in he said, 'If things – if things don't go right, you could telephone me.'

'You don't need to worry.'

'I shall worry.'

'I said you don't need to.'

She wouldn't let him kiss her but she took his hand and held it looking up into his face. 'Don't stay alone for too long, it's bad for you.'

'You have a nerve to give anybody advice.'

'The fact that I've made a mess of my own life so far doesn't stop me seeing where other people go wrong.'

'I could advertise,' he said. 'Perhaps it would be more satisfactory if I just bought a dog.'

'Some women make very good dogs.'

She got into the train behind a stout man and when he became wedged by his suitcases in the corridor, she smiled at Venniker through the window; she seemed to have herself under absolute control, to have gained in assurance even in the hour or so since they had left Larche. Her last words, shouted as the train pulled out, were that he should say good-bye to Aldo for her.

After she had gone, he drank a few cognacs and wandered round shops, looking for things that would make a difference to life at Larche. Eventually he bought some tubing and brushes for cleaning out the kitchen drain. He imagined the sense of freedom he would feel if he could be patient enough. He felt very slightly sick.

Rattling back to the gatehouse at noon, he had almost passed through the lavender when he saw Aldo straighten up from the crop and raise an arm. He got out of the 2CV and walked over.

'The gendarme from Mersac was here earlier.'

'Jules? Did he say what he wanted?'

'Only that he hadn't seen you about in Mersac and wondered if you had gone away on a trip.'

Curiosity, Venniker thought, the mark of a good policeman anywhere. Presumably Jules had been warned by his head-quarters about Seagram's visit, had even perhaps been required to submit a report for sending on to the Yard. And perhaps too he had seen Daye with Opal and found that interesting enough for a five minutes call on a quiet morning's round.

'No questions?'

'No.' Aldo looked him in the eyes and then back towards the gatehouse. There was nothing to announce the fact but Venniker felt he had guessed that Opal had gone.

'How is your mother?'

'She is much better today.'

'Come and have a glass of wine.'

'Thank you. I shall finish in ten minutes. I will come then.'

Venniker left the car under the chestnut tree where, he had agreed with Opal, it would never be parked. In the gatehouse waiting for Aldo to appear, he went up to the bedroom to make sure Opal had left nothing behind. The Vivaldi she had bought when they made their first visit together to Cahors was on the turntable of the record player. He took it off and fitted it into its sleeve. Then he threw it under the bed, where the bills were.

12

The days that followed were still and oppressive, the clouds banking up as they rolled over from the Atlantic but never quite releasing their contents on the *causse*. Venniker worked in the apricot orchard and finished the roof of the *pigeonnier*. Nobody came except Aldo, not even the post van. Going occasionally to the shops in Mersac he found himself lingering more and more at the tables outside the café, talking to anyone who would pass the time with him. Opal was never mentioned but they all knew she had gone. On the day he drew the money Seagram had sent to the Credit Agricole he stayed so late at the hotel, Madame turned him out. On his way back to Larche he was sick in a ditch, and stayed there the night.

Finally, the telephone rang. It was a woman's voice speaking English. For a moment he thought this was Opal adopting a crisper, more incisive tone to deceive him. But when she spoke a second time he dismissed the possibility.

'You know who this is . . . ?'

It was early evening but he was already thick with wine. 'No.' Then suddenly, he was back in the hotel room in Brussels and he remembered her mouth moving upon him and the coming alive again. 'Yes.'

'I should like to see you. Are you by yourself?'

'Yes.'

'No girl friend?'

'She's left.'

'So if I come, I can be sure there will be no one about . . .'

'Of course. But where *are* you?'

'Quite near. I'll be with you in about half an hour.'

When he replaced the receiver he cursed and then laughed, his reactions wholly at odds. Excitement began to stir in his stomach.

It was more like an hour by the time he heard a car coming down the track. At a guess Françoise must have called him from near Cahors, assuming she had driven from the north. From the open door of the gatehouse he watched the headlights move alongside the 2CV under the chestnut tree and then fade. A figure materialized out of midsummer darkness. As she came within the light of the lamp behind him, he saw she was dressed in white trousers and shirt, both immaculate. She had something of the air of a tourist visiting the Great Outdoors from some comfortable bourgeois apartment in Paris. After his initial surprise, he realized the effect was deliberate, the sort of contemptuous disguise he could imagine appealing to her. But the leather bag slung over her shoulder was the same one that had held the gun in Brussels.

In the kitchen she threw the bag on the table and looked round, smiling. 'I like this.' She took a cigarette from his pack and sat down to light it.

'Have you driven all the way from Brussels?' he asked.

'Yes, but in stages. Could I have something to eat? The last meal I had was in Paris.'

He opened a tin of meat and found some wrinkled tomatoes to add to a lettuce. As he sat down to watch her eat Françoise said, as though he was being called to account, 'Tell me how you live. What do you do all day long?'

He gave her an account of his industry, slightly exaggerated. She listened attentively, questioned him often, pushing fingers through the cropped black hair while she made sure she was asking him precisely what interested her. When she had finished eating she said, 'The pigeon-house, where the tunnel is – does one approach it by the same track I drove along?'

'Yes, there's a fork near the barn. Another track goes off. Are you planning to look in the dark?'

'No,' she said. 'Tomorrow. Tomorrow morning will do.' So there was no doubt left as to what she intended for the night.

It was better than in Brussels because this time he had self-confidence that was the equal of hers. She uttered no words, acknowledged nothing except with her body, but he saw in her eyes the gluttony that, for all her assurance in other ways, would make her vulnerable perhaps at moments when she needed not to be.

In the morning, before the sun touched the windows, they lay and listened to the hens and the peacocks waking up. Finally she sat up and looked at her watch. 'In two hours I must leave.'

'How far are you going?'

'Back to the north. About eight hours driving – perhaps more.'

'You never answer questions properly.'

She shrugged and asked for a towel so that she could shower. He pointed to a drawer and watched her as she searched, pushing aside a pair of pants Opal had failed to pack. She showed no interest at all. While she was in the hut he went through the pockets of the shirt and trousers she had arrived in, drawing the same blank as in Brussels. She had taken the bag with her.

Over coffee and the stale bread from yesterday she asked him about the Lot, and why it was also called Quercy.

'It's the old name – from the Latin for an oak tree.'

'Did you learn Latin at school?'

'Latin and Ancient Greek were the staple diet.'

'A classical man,' she said. 'My God.' She smiled with a sour sort of amusement. For the first time he saw plainly what vanity had encouraged him to ignore – that while he interested her physically, his rating was otherwise tepid. '*You* arranged to be taught only what you wanted, did you?' he said.

Françoise shrugged. 'I had the usual *petit bourgeois* pap. But they wouldn't have got away with stuffing me with dead languages.'

He thought then how much he would enjoy telling her what he knew about her, of how he might say – so exactly *when* was it that Gail Landon decided the pap had been so nauseating there was only one way of making up for it: pushing drugs and blowing things up and calling it all HANGMAN? 'Bully for you,' he said.

After he had shown her the tunnel, she stood leaning against the outside of the *pigeonnier*, picking at his new mortar with a fingernail and memorizing the geography about her. Finally she said, 'It will suit very well.'

'How?'

'We shall use it for various things. In return you'll be paid

1000 francs a month. You don't need to know more. So far as you are concerned, you've been told it is a temporary store for antique furniture which is going to be restored and then exported. Stuff that has been collected in different parts of the Lot.'

'What does it involve me doing?'

'Nothing. Just keep other people out of the store. We shall fit a lock and not give you a key so that should be easy for you. Once or perhaps twice a month a truck will arrive. It will always be at night. The truck will be gone well before daybreak.'

'Why does your store have to be in this area?'

'It's quiet, close to good roads, reasonably central for our purposes.' She paused, then smiled briefly. 'I also have a reason of my own for preferring your place.'

She was looking into the distance and he knew that whatever she was thinking about had nothing to do with himself. 'It's a long way from Brussels,' he said.

She pulled her shoulder bag in front of her and opened it. 'The supplies we shall be storing here have nothing to do with Brussels. Their destination is also different.' She took a roll of French franc notes from the bag and counted off ten one hundreds. 'We should like to pay you a month in advance.'

He let her go on holding the money. 'I'm not sure about this. Why should I involve myself without knowing more of the actual risk I'm running?'

'Because it's money for nothing. Because the risk is minimal. And because you're already involved. You've already worked for us and found that we are very careful and quite generous about money. Your fat friend can bear witness to that.'

It was a moment or two before he realized she was talking about the former Moley Jewkes, only begetter of Rex Arundel. That was it, of course; from her point of view he was just another Moley. He folded the notes and put them in his pocket. 'All right. Who will bring the truck?'

'There will usually be two of us. Sometimes I shall come.' She placed her hand on his cheek, then moved it slowly down.

She had it all worked out, like a salesman loose in a new city, matching carnal pursuit to the business schedule. When she let her hand drop, he said, 'You might look at my view before you go. It's quite pretty.'

He took her round the back of the *pigeonnier* and beyond until they reached what had been the terrace of the château, running along the edge of the cliff. Across the valley the roofs of Mersac were a hazy pink in the early morning sun.

She nodded. 'Very pretty. But perhaps a little boring. And rather dead.'

'Not always. Once upon a time looking across at that tower you'd have noticed something not at all boring. Even though it *was* dead.'

He told her the story of the German officer nailed to the pole under the Red flag. She listened carefully.

'What else can you tell me about those times here?' she asked.

'Nothing much.'

'Try to remember.'

He racked his brain for anecdotes picked up at monthly visits to the barber in Mersac or when listening to the old men at the tables outside the café. 'Why are you so interested?'

'It's an indulgence, a certain weakness. It relates to those times. Someone who knows me calls it my Achilles heel.'

It was the first occasion he could recall her acknowledging weakness. But precisely what she meant was a mystery. 'If you'd asked me, I would have said your indulgence was preferring to talk in riddles.'

'It's unimportant anyway.' She turned to him. 'Don't you ever want to get out of here and *do* things?'

'What for example?'

'Leave some mark on the world. Influence it, change it. Or, if not the world, at least that part you can see over there. Don't you feel it's a waste just to hide away here?'

'I might if I *were* hiding. But I'm not. I've left my mark "over there", as you say. Now I'm doing it here. Except that I prefer it here, there's really no difference.' He tried touching her with the knife himself. 'You may come to the same conclusion yourself one day.'

'But what have you actually *done* here?'

He looked back at the *pigeonnier*. From this side the new stonework presented its most botched appearance. It was where he had started the rebuilding work. He laughed. 'Not much you'd understand.'

Her eyes had followed his but she had stopped being interested in what he was saying. 'Next week or the one after could be the most important one in my life – and for many others. Everything could begin to change – everything. That's what I mean when I talk of doing things.'

As they walked to her car Venniker said, 'This someone who knows you well enough to recognize your Achilles heel – is he one of the two other people you told me that you trust?'

'Yes.'

'A partner?'

'If you like.'

'Is *he* also waiting for next week or the one after?'

'Yes.'

He tried one more cast over the water, one more hook. 'What I wish you'd explain to me is why you're into crime at all. It doesn't seem to fit. What do you want out of it?'

'What do people usually go into crime for?'

'You know damn well it's not money in your case.'

She wrinkled her nose at bird droppings on the seat of the open Peugeot she was driving. 'I said we'd talk one day. When I'm convinced you'll understand I'll tell you.' It sounded pretty condescending. Yet he still couldn't forget there was something else to her that had made him more alive than he had been for a long time.

She spread a duster on the droppings, seated herself and then climbed out of the car again for a final trip to the bathroom. Several 1/200000 Michelin maps and a sweater lay on the passenger seat. He opened the glove box and found more maps, all of France and Belgium. Right at the back was a screwed-up piece of newsprint that must have been folded amongst the maps at one time. The language was English and one passage was sidelined in ink. On impulse he slipped it into his pocket.

When she returned to the car he asked, 'When will the truck come?'

'I'm not sure. But we shall probably telephone you beforehand to make sure there are no problems – no visitors.'

He had a mental flash of Opal walking slowly towards him carrying the soft-top suitcase along the track out of the orchard, but he didn't believe it. 'I don't think there'll be any problems,' he said. He picked up a peacock feather and handed it to her. 'A souvenir from Old Quercy. One day when you're franker with me, I may tell you what that means.'

Back in the house he booked a call to Seagram and went into the bedroom to make the bed. This time he could feel her in every corner of the room, found himself going back in his mind over and over again the way it had been. It was a unique excitement that she gave him, something he had never experienced with any other woman. Already he knew an inconvenient fact: that he hoped he would have her at least once more before Seagram intervened.

The telephone rang within the hour. It was the switchboard girl in Mersac to tell him that the operators in the International Exchange in London were all on strike and no forecast could be made for when his connection might come through. He thought: to hell with Seagram, let him wait anyway. I'm doing all his bloody work. Haven't I got more important things to think about?

After a while, he decided what they might be: the vine needed spraying; and if he didn't burn his refuse pile today it would have grown twice as high as the ring of stones that held it together.

The yellow post van drove up as he was returning from the blaze, the smell of burning plastic bottles everywhere. For once it brought something other than a bill, a postcard of a top-heavy girl lying on a beach in the bottom half of a bikini. On the other side Opal had written, 'Sending her on by parcel post ... Hope the hens are laying. The lap of luxury here, fantastic garden, swimming pool to myself, resident cook who asks twice a day what I want for next meal, etc. J.D. away, wheeling and dealing somewhere. Think of me sometimes. I think of you. Opal.'

Going to the apricot orchard he tossed the postcard amongst the smouldering pile of rubbish en route. He half-knew it was a game with himself, an exploration to find out if he cared that between the lines on the postcard he had sensed she was miserable.

By evening, he had reached a decision and didn't find it too wounding to his dignity. To hell with the apricots for forty-eight hours; after he had seen Aldo tomorrow, he would take a holiday, no harm in pointing the 2CV in the general direction of Cap Ferrat; no harm in looking up Opal. And no harm in letting Seagram wait that long.

When he was eating his supper he unfolded the piece of newsprint he had found in the glove box of Françoise's car. It was, he deduced from the heading, torn from a Sussex county newspaper. One side contained a cosy piece on Japanese flower-arranging; on the other, where the ink marks were, was an article about a West Sussex village. The village was Pakeham and there were colour photographs to prove it. The side-lined paragraphs had a flavour he couldn't recall tasting since, as a boy, he had thumbed wearily through the *Bedgley Chronicle*.

Opposite the fifteenth-century church stands Bay Tree Cottage, now for sale since its former owner, Miss Christie, died recently at the grand age of ninety-seven. Bay Tree Cottage, with its wistaria-clad beams and lattice windows, stands sentinel at the top of Church Hill, watching, one may imagine, for the dwindling number of vehicles that still are tempted by the old London road from the coast in preference to the by-pass. Legend has it that the cottage was the house of the village cobbler in medieval times and the carving of a boot over the great inglenook may bear witness to this.

But by the reign of Queen Anne, Bay Tree Cottage had become a clearing-house for smugglers of cognac from France. The barrels, it seems, were rolled down a shaft on the lane beside the churchyard into an underground room. From there they were moved into a secret inner chamber in case Her Majesty's Customs officers were minded to make a call. In more recent times other liquor that would not have caused the Customs and Excise quite such concern was stored there – Miss Christie's highly-prized damson wine!

Some words had been written in French next to the side-lining. '*Vingt kilometres de la côte. Tranquil.*'

He laughed, gazing at the place where the Peugeot had been parked. What was that about petit bourgeois pap, he said aloud.

That night, disappointingly, he dreamed of Miss Christie. She was knocking back the damson wine.

13

Emerging at last from dusty suburban entrails into the centre of Nice, Venniker found himself among arcaded buildings, cool bars and barber shops, and *fin de siècle* villas walled away in secret gardens. Flowers erupted from balconies and tubs. Women sauntered, softly brown.

Halted finally short of the Promenade des Anglais by an impenetrable jam of traffic, he left the Citroen to stretch his legs and buy nougat from a roadside stall. On either side of the stall two great palm trees reared like Masai warriors, their feathered heads moving in a private breeze.

After the oven heat of the journey, Nice was an oasis. Something of the excitement of his first arrival in London came back to Venniker, that distinctive metropolitan thrill. But here, unlike London, it was all under sun that made the shoddiest apartments glisten and gave an honest truth to shade.

It took another forty minutes to arrive at Cap Ferrat. Finding Jay Daye's villa was harder than he had expected. In shops and cafés he was met by shaking heads when he mentioned Daye's name; it was only when he spoke of the ruby ear-rings that somebody grinned and told him the way.

The villa he had been directed to, at the end of a cul-de-sac, was a mild surprise. It had been built, he judged, at the end of the nineteenth century, a tallish terracotta house, with long grey shutters and a pantiled roof on two or three levels. The site, the size and condition of the grounds, the elaborate iron gates at the entrance, all guaranteed it had cost a lot of money. But its gaunt and faded appearance seemed too austere for someone of Daye's kind.

Both the iron gates and the front door of the house were open. He stepped into a high, silent chamber, empty of furniture except along the sides so that the eye fell first on a floor of white and cinnamon mosaic, with remotely pastoral beings coupling at its heart. The walls were *faux marbre* broken by dark varnished doors tall enough for giants. A memory just out of reach teased him for a moment or two until he caught it at last. He was back in the food hall at Harrods.

Systematically he went round the rooms on the ground floor. They were all empty of life except for the kitchen, in which a Spanish-looking woman was asleep in a basket chair. He hesitated by the staircase and then decided to try the garden first.

The area close to the house looked as though it had been re-planned recently. A swimming-pool lay twenty yards from Venniker across a terrace that had french doors directly overlooking the sea. At the far end of the pool were twin pavilions with bougainvillea and blue cactus massed behind. One of the pavil-ions was in shade; beside the other, on a reclining chair the colour of emerald, lay Opal. She wore the wide-brimmed straw hat he had bought her in Cahors market, sunglasses and bikini pants.

Although her head was erect and turned towards him, she must have had her eyes closed or been day-dreaming; she didn't see him until he had almost reached her. Then she started violently. 'Paul . . .!'

He grinned at her astonishment.

'How . . . ?'

'I decided on a change of air. It seemed polite to call – since I was in the neighbourhood.'

He moved to the pool edge to see her in profile. She had filled out more. All the muscle tone was back. Full sun on the flesh and a build-up of the tan had combined to complete the miracle. She looked, he thought, sensational.

He handed her the box of nougat. 'Specially blended with exhaust fumes. You try it first.'

She was still getting over her surprise. 'If you've driven straight down from Larche you must be gasping. Do you want a swim?'

Venniker gazed down into the water. It looked as grubby as he felt; the filtration system must be on the blink. 'It seems very murky. Doesn't Daye worry about little matters of hygiene?'

'He's away.'

'There must be servants who know about cleaning it surely.'

'The gardener looks after the pool but he's gone off sick. There's only the cook at the moment.'

He sat down beside her outstretched legs. 'You don't find it lonely?'

'No. It's marvellous just waking up each day and knowing that the only problem is whether to go to the beach or stay here.'

She wasn't altogether convincing. On the other hand he could see she was not really unhappy. He said, 'I somehow imagined Jay Daye with rather more of an entourage than a cook and a gardener.'

'He keeps this place just for himself. I suppose the others could be in the Fontainebleau house – that's where he's staying now. His current boy's with him.'

'Is that his main preoccupation – small boys?'

'Not small – this one must be at least twenty-five. Half-French, half-Italian. It's a Big Thing. In the study you'll find a blown-up photograph of him covering one wall. See if he turns you on.'

'I don't think I'll risk it.'

She smiled. Venniker put his hand on her thigh, moved the fingers over and out of memory. 'All right?'

'Fine.'

'You look terrific.'

'It's terrific seeing *you*.'

He knew what she was saying: let's behave as though those things between us the day before I left never happened. But that wasn't what really concerned him. Did she want to say – after all, I need you? And did he want her to say it?

'Has Daye got you any work?'

'Not yet. I'd only been here two days when he had to go off on one of his trips. I think he must intend to become a tycoon. It would be a way of proving himself, of showing the world that an ex-pop singer can count in other ways.'

'You're studying the inner man then ...' He just avoided sneering.

'I don't think I'd find it very attractive if I did.'

'Have you slept with him since that time at Larche?'

'No.'

He believed her, he didn't know why. After a while he took his hand away from her thigh. She reached out and clasped his fingers. 'Tell me about things at Larche.'

'I've sprayed half the apricots. Aldo is suffering from piles. It's all go.'

'Nothing else?'

'No. You left a pair of pants behind. But perhaps you don't need them too much here.' He stood up, uncertain of himself, suddenly tense. 'Perhaps I'll have a look round inside. It's not often I visit the house of a man worth a million pounds. How does one *make* a million pounds?'

'By being motivated.' She was getting at him.

He wandered into the house and took the stairs. The rooms above had obviously been done by an interior decorator who hadn't liked what he saw on the ground floor. There were swagged curtains, long-haired rugs, vanitory fitments and lots of mirrors. The guest bedrooms had French Empire beds and drinks cupboards with marquetry fronts beside the beds; in Daye's own room the bed was a round jumbo. Beardsley seemed to be the favoured filling for spaces on the walls.

Downstairs again Venniker went into the study to gaze on the mural photograph of Daye's boy. It was a nude torso shot, the skin apparently oiled; the lighting was reminiscent of an old German movie. He looked into the face. Behind the mask of self-absorption, the bar boy sultriness, there was a hint of something more interesting, an intelligence perhaps, trying to find a way through.

There was a writing desk beneath the photograph with a leather bound blotting pad, unused; the pigeon-holes were also empty; there were no pens or pencils. The whole thing appeared untouched like most of the articles in the room. Venniker tried the desk drawers, knowing they would be just the same, all part of a furnishing job for a theatrical set. Yet one was different, even contained an authentic personal possession. It was an album of whipping pictures, the subjects of varied sorts and sizes, mostly girls; they were chained or bound in a fancy way. The inscription in the front of the album said: 'To Jay, from Lee, Caffy and Peke – Happy Xmas!'

Opal had just emerged from the pool when Venniker got back to the terrace. She stood shaking water out of her hair. 'You've been a long time.'

'I wanted to do it justice.'

'Impressed?'

He gazed at trickles taking a wayward path over her breasts and wondered if he would desire her as much as he did at this moment if she didn't seem almost out of reach. 'I liked the bathrooms. Otherwise I don't think it comes up to Larche.'

'You love Larche, don't you?' she said.

'I think I do.'

They sat on a swing seat under a canopy at the other end of the terrace. She kissed his face quickly and then went on drying herself. It was a sibling occasion, he thought, except for her nakedness.

He took her hand. 'There's something I have to say. I don't know whether you'll listen or care.' He hesitated because the words were going to sound ridiculous; but he couldn't think of any others. He felt the water from her skin creeping through his slacks. 'Whatever Daye has promised to do for you I don't rate this a good place from your point of view.'

'Why not?'

'Daye isn't the open-hearted sort. It's not his form, disinterestedly offering bed and board and introductions to the design industry.'

'But that's exactly what he is doing.'

'There's got to be a pay-off.'

'I've paid,' she said, 'with my Body.' She rolled her eyes and looked dramatic; she wasn't going to listen to him.

'He also likes tricks that wouldn't suit you. Unpleasant tricks.'

'If you've been looking at the album in the desk, don't worry, I've seen it. He knows I wouldn't play.'

'He might not give you any choice one night when he's bored with his beautiful boy.'

'Paul, I can look after myself now. I really can. You have to accept that.'

Dispirited, he turned his head away from her. 'Right,' he said.

Shade had reached the second of the pavilions at the end of the swimming pool. The air would soon be cooler. He could climb into the 2CV and head back for Larche now. Or he could spend the night in Nice. Either way he was going to feel low.

'Paul,' she said again. He shook his head. Her voice was down to a whisper. 'I could go back with you – if you're lonely.'

'Do you think that's why I came?'

'No.' She had reddened. 'I just felt you *were* – lonely.'

She reached for his hand again. 'I got things wrong when we had that quarrel. It seemed then that if I stopped being a mess and stood on my own feet, you wouldn't get any charge out of me. I thought – this is hopeless. I've thought about it since I've been here. I don't believe that now.'

He watched a bird fly a rising and dipping course across the terrace to explore for insects in a blue clematis. He thought: *you* may not believe it but unfortunately that isn't quite enough. It takes two to tango. And the plain truth is, you were right in the first place. I don't know that it *does* work for me if the other person in the relationship isn't a bit damaged. To be more exact, if you came back, I'm scared I might prove that.

Perhaps Jay Daye's taste for whipping was only a more spectacular version of his own kink. They both needed to have people who were damaged. He stood up. 'That wasn't why I came. I wanted to be sure you were all right. You've convinced me.'

'You're not answering me.'

He took a deep breath. 'I'm not lonely. What I want is for you to make it. Trying in Jay Daye's company strikes me as more than a little bizarre. But I could be wrong. At least you know the score. Just keep safe. All right?'

'Are you being honest?'

'I *am* saying what I mean.' He glanced at his watch. 'You could pour some of Daye's scotch down me before I go.'

Opal was frowning up at him as though trying to read his face. Then she smiled rather mechanically and shrugged. 'I'll get the scotch. You could still have a swim while you're waiting.'

He didn't know what she really thought and it didn't matter now. He watched her until she disappeared through the french doors, then took off his clothes and dived into the water. Opening his eyes as he tried a width below the surface, he saw its depths were surprisingly clear; the pool was in a better condition than it had seemed, when he had viewed it from above. On the tiles at the bottom of the deep end he noticed a sandal and recognized it for one Opal had worn in Rome. Picking it up he surfaced and threw the sandal high in the air towards the villa. It fell short, disappearing into shrubbery. Watching its flight he felt that nothing would come out right ever again.

He was almost through Nice on the road north when he decided finally that he couldn't face a night alone. Turning the car about, he drove back to the centre of the town, looking for the right sort of hotel. He found one on a wide boulevard, with its bar opening on to gardens at the front. Inside there were rather more locals than tourists; two girls were operating the place. Occasionally exchanging brief words, they sipped their drinks and made small reconnaissances in and out of the gardens.

He booked a room and returned to the bar, making for the nearest girl. She greeted him as though it was an assignation they had had in their minds all day. He agreed to her price without a moment's thought.

It was a night for trying anything. Lying on the bed while she was in the bathroom, he picked up the phone and for the hell of it asked the hotel exchange to get him Scotland Yard. To his surprise he was speaking to Seagram's office before the bathroom door opened again. Seagram himself was not there, although expected back later. He refused to leave a message. 'Just tell him to telephone me on this number tonight. It's important to him.'

The sergeant at the other end tried saying he wasn't certain it would be possible. 'Fine,' he said, 'his loss not mine.' As he replaced the receiver, he began to feel better. When the girl came in, he looked at her for a long time, answering her smile without speaking. 'You look happy,' she said.

'I want you to have dinner with me and then stay on. I'll treble the money.'

'If you wish.' She was just a little guarded but he didn't blame her for that.

He let her choose the restaurant and she took him to one in the old town where there weren't any tourists, although the prices were no better for that. He noticed she stayed on Vichy water until half-way through the meal when she must have decided it really was going to be an easy night and she could relax. As she raised her glass of burgundy he said, 'Drink to the beautiful people. Ourselves.' 'To us,' she said. She had a charming and immediate smile that seemed entirely unforced. He said, 'I admire you very much. I was a professional once but hardly in your league.' She laughed and rounded her eyes suitably but he judged she didn't believe him.

They had scarcely undressed back at the hotel when the telephone rang. It was Seagram. 'Something happened?'

'Not yet. But it will. Meanwhile I'm in Nice having a little break from shouldering your burdens. I'm in bed with a charming friend.'

Seagram said tightly, 'Perhaps you'd like me to telephone when your friend has left.'

He realized that he probably sounded drunk. The girl lay with her head on the pillow beside him. He reached an arm out to her. 'I tried to telephone you yesterday. As usual you had somebody on strike over there and I couldn't get through. My Brussels girl friend – not the one who's with me now of course – has made contact. Not only that, she's arranged to store stuff at my place.'

'Definitely?'

'Definitely. So I'd very much like the French police told the score in case they get on to it independently.'

'Of course.' Seagram's voice had changed, it was both pleased and conciliatory. 'We'll arrange that, don't worry.'

'When?'

'Pretty soon, Paul.'

'Why not now?'

'Just as soon as we've got clearance to go ahead from the big man.'

'Do you mean you're *still* waiting for that?'

'There's a diplomatic complication – you heard what he said at the meeting. I can't ignore that and go my own way. We have to live with politicians like everybody else.'

The girl was watching Venniker's face as he talked; he wondered how much she understood of what he was saying. 'You may have to live with them,' he said, 'I don't. But I *do* need to keep my nose clean in Mersac with my friend Jules, the gendarme.'

'When will the stuff arrive?'

'She didn't say. I'll be warned by telephone beforehand.'

'Let me know the minute you hear more. In the meantime I guarantee I'll get the Commissioner to go and see the Home Secretary again.'

He sighed. 'All right. Have you dug up anything interesting since I saw you?'

Seagram hesitated fractionally. 'One small thing. It only helps to fill in the background but it's useful. The last HANG-MAN bombing was five days ago at the house of Lord Bayes who, in case you've forgotten, is a big financier. Two bombs were used at different points of the house – it's a bloody great mansion – but only one went off. The Bomb Squad were able to recover the other bomb intact.'

'So you've got fingerprints ...'

'No such luck. But what we do have are sticks of gelignite stamped with the date of manufacture and the factory in France they came from. The interesting thing is that the factory happens to be one that cropped up in the Angry Brigade investigation. So we're beginning to see HANGMAN a bit more clearly. What we may be dealing with are some nuts who were mixed up with that group but who never got caught.'

The girl disengaged from Venniker's arm and went to pick up some of her clothing that had slipped from a chair to the floor. She folded it briskly, walked to the door and clicked out the overhead light. Round one ankle was a silver chain; it occurred to Venniker that he had not seen one of those for twenty years.

'Well, that's all,' said Seagram.

'Yes,' he said and then suddenly remembered. 'No, there *is* one other item for you. It may or may not be a lead. It's a newspaper article I took from Françoise's car when she wasn't looking. Something in it might just relate to storage plans in England. I'll put it into an envelope as soon as I get back to Larche tomorrow.'

When he replaced the receiver, the girl said, 'You sound very important.'

He smiled, not disposed to disillusion her.

'Are you a police agent?'

So she had understood quite a lot. 'Now and then.'

She kissed him here and there to show how impressed she was. 'No more calls.'

'No more calls.'

He woke very early the following day. Returning to bed from the bathroom, he paused by the window and looked down at the hotel garden. White chairs and tables glimmered in the light from the lamps on the boulevard. A cat was sitting like a night-watchman by the gate. Along the side of the garden, palm trees as tall as those he had noticed by the nougat-stand the day before reached for heaven. Up and up they went like totems, prodding the sky with their feathered butts.

The girl was asleep with her lips slightly apart. Unlike Opal she slept neatly, purposefully, as though she had folded herself away in tissue to be fresh for the next round. He kissed the nape of her neck; it was very pale and cool – the only part of her that struck him as seeming vulnerable.

14

Brown water had begun to belch back through the sink waste as a reminder that the drain outside the kitchen was still on strike, when the call came through. The time was eleven o'clock. He would have been in bed if he had not been chilling his blood by reading up the symptoms of rust on the apricots.

He picked up the telephone receiver and Françoise's voice said briskly, 'In half an hour. All right?'

Silently he cursed Seagram. Presumably the fact he had heard nothing since he had spoken to him from Nice meant that the Commissioner and the Home Secretary were still dancing a minuet. 'All right,' he said, 'who ...?' But she had already disconnected.

He went outside and poked at the drain for a while by the light of his torch. The blockage began to loosen. As he straightened up, he heard an engine approaching along the track through the orchard. Not more than a quarter of an hour had gone by since Françoise's call; she must have been in or very near Mersac. The vehicle stopped where the path to the *pigeonnier* divided from the main track and the headlights went out. After a few moments he saw a light moving down through the trees towards the *pigeonnier*. He watched for its return, supposing that would signal the beginning of the operation of transferring stuff to the tunnel. But nothing happened. For five minutes he stood staring into the darkness without reward.

Curiosity finally impelled him to a reconnaissance. Making his way along the grass to the right of the track, he approached the spot where the vehicle had stopped. In one of the apertures of the *pigeonnier* a light was showing. Françoise and whoever else had come with her were presumably inside. He switched on his torch.

The vehicle was a green van, windowless at the sides and

rear. He opened the loading doors at the back and shone the torch beam inside. There were half a dozen cardboard boxes. He opened the nearest; it was empty. He tried another and then another – all empty. Killing the torch, he shut the doors. He could go down to the *pigeonnier*; but there was no way of seeing inside without opening the door and such obvious interference would certainly arouse Françoise's suspicions. A cicada chirped, lonely for company. Almost in the same moment the cool tip of a gun barrel touched his neck behind the ear. '*Ne bougez point*,' a man said in not very good French. The torch was removed from Venniker's fingers and its beam clicked on a few inches from his face.

There was a pause which he found uncomfortable; the man was possibly examining his features. The cicada tried again. Eventually the man said in English hardly better than his French, 'Very well, Venniker, you can turn round now.'

Venniker looked behind him. He could see nothing of the man's face beyond the glare of the torch. The voice had sounded fairly young. He said, 'I suppose you're with Françoise.'

'Yes.'

'Why the gun?'

'I was not sure who you were.' The accent was either Dutch or German.

'I saw the light and came to look. I couldn't understand why you didn't call at the house to say you'd arrived.'

'We didn't want to disturb you unnecessarily.' The tone of voice was very slightly insulting. Venniker moved to the side, a little away from the torch beam, but he could still see nothing of the man's features. 'You've unloaded already then . . .'

'Why do you say that?'

'I took a glance inside the van.' Better to come out with it since the man had probably seen him anyway.

'That was very inquisitive.' The man was sliding the gun into his waistband. 'No, we decided on what you call a dry run. There has been nothing unloaded. We wanted to check timings. And to see how the visit would work out – whether anything unpleasant would be waiting.' He spoke the last few words very slowly as though he might not be understood otherwise.

'So what is Françoise doing?'

'She is fitting a new lock to your cellar door. She enjoys using her hands. But you have of course discovered that, Venniker.' He didn't sound jealous, just sour and contemptuous. Switching off the torch he pushed it into Venniker's hand again. 'I suggest you wait for us in the house. We shall call before we leave.'

There was obviously no point in standing there. 'As you like,' he said, 'but if you've not arrived in a quarter of an hour, I'm going to bed – I've had a busy day.' He walked back to the gatehouse. It still felt uncomfortable having his back to the man.

He had poured himself a cognac and was trying to get back to apricot rust when they appeared in the doorway of the kitchen. They were wearing black shirts, black jeans and black canvas shoes. 'I hadn't realized it was quite such a formal occasion,' he said. As the man stepped into the lamplight, he saw his features properly at last, the narrow cheeks, the spectacles with transparent frames, the pale blond hair. Recognition flashed into his mind so instantaneously he almost smiled. 'Oh,' he said. 'You.' The man said nothing.

He gave them drinks. Françoise had taken out a cigarette. As Venniker lit it for her, their eyes levelled. She smiled economically. 'How are you, Paul?'

He bowed slightly. 'How are *you*?' All the buttons of her shirt were done up. She looked very operational.

Her companion wandered about the room with his cognac. He stopped at the wall near the door to the sitting-room and peered at the John Leech hunting scene that had belonged to Venniker's father. 'Very British,' he said. 'And where do you keep your other paintings?'

'What paintings?'

'Those you try to sell.'

He felt a coldness, as though the gun barrel was back against his neck. Somehow he had dismissed the art forgery ploy from his mind after it had served its purpose in the opening move with Jewkes. 'I'm waiting for a fresh supply.' He reached for the cognac bottle. 'When are you actually going to bring some of *your* stock in trade? Or is that to remain a great secret?'

'Soon enough.'

'We ought to agree on a code,' Françoise said, 'for when we telephone you.'

'Ikons,' said the blond man, 'the ikons are ready for delivery. How about that, Venniker?' His eyes were empty of expression.

'The girl on the local switchboard who listens to most of the calls when she isn't busy would find that rather odd. I think you'd better tell me you're on your way to talk about the lavender. Everybody in Mersac knows I've failed to sell it so far.'

'Lavender.' The man yawned and then shrugged. 'All right. Now I should like to use your lavatory.'

'If the open air doesn't attract, you'd better take my torch. Ten paces to the left from the kitchen door, down eight steps then turn right. Don't frighten the bats – they've just settled in above the cistern.'

When he had gone, Venniker said to Françoise 'Your friend came into the Café Grand' Place in Brussels the night Jewkes took me there. He sat down at the same table as you and behaved as though he had never seen you before in his life. Right?'

'Correct.'

'Looking me over?'

'Yes.'

'Wasn't it rather superfluous for both of you to be doing the same thing?'

'We like to make independent judgements when we are thinking of employing new people.'

'Was it his idea that tonight's trip should be a dry run?'

She looked irritated, even a little bored. 'This is no concern of yours.'

'You make a great thing about being cautious and checking everything. But it wasn't very sensible telephoning when you'd almost got here. Supposing the local policeman had been making a call?'

'We had made other arrangements to be sure the coast was clear.' Françoise smiled, then shrugged. Moving to him she placed her mouth on his in an exploratory way. When she drew back, she said, 'Next time I stay. Next time.'

He wondered what she would do with her blond friend. But that was her problem, not his. 'I'll look forward to that,' he said. He sat on the edge of the table and considered the fastenings of her shirt. 'I can't say I feel your partner displays unqualified confidence in me.'

'He's suspicious by nature. You don't have to take it personally. It's very important to us – our security.'

'He sounds German. Is he?'

Françoise nodded unwillingly. 'Yes.'

'One of the two people you once told me you trusted ...?'

'Yes.'

'Well, well,' he said. 'I hope you know best.'

'I know enough.' Her self confidence was impregnable.

The blond man came back and tossed off the rest of his drink. Looking at Françoise, he said, 'I think perhaps we should leave.'

Venniker stood up and stretched. 'I would hate you to suppose I was being over-inquisitive again, but am I going to be told your name? If not, I shall just go on thinking of you as the Kraut.'

He saw a tinge of colour rising at the side of the man's neck. So he could bleed. There was a small pause. Françoise said, 'You can call him Saul.' She was smiling in a curious way.

'Saul?'

'Yes.'

The blond man frowned briefly, not in a particularly disapproving way but as though he had had genuine difficulty in understanding her; or perhaps he was just surprised she had given any answer at all. Then he looked resigned. Whatever his first reaction he had decided it didn't matter much. 'Let's go,' he said to Françoise.

Venniker opened the door for them. 'You're surely not driving all the way back to Brussels in that thing?'

Françoise said, 'No.'

'Then – what ...?'

'It's not being driven as far as Brussels.' She never gave anything away.

He made an abrupt decision; looking back afterwards it seemed as though the decision had taken possession of him, not the other way round. Reaching to take his jacket down from behind the door and picking up the torch, he said, 'I'll light you back to the van.'

He waited for them both to get seated in the front of the van, flashed the torch against the rear doors and then called to Saul, sitting at the wheel. 'Hold on, the doors don't look fastened.' Moving round the back he opened them, rattling the handle, swung his body on to the floor of the rear compartment and, with his head still outside, shouted, 'O.K. now, see you soon.' Pulling the doors gently inwards, he offered up a prayer.

His first fear was that Saul would engage gear so quickly after he had called out that he would be thrown against the doors as the van pulled away. But all was well: the German gave the accelerator a preliminary burst before moving off; as the engine raced Venniker had time to secure the door catch and brace himself against the side of the van ready for the potholes in the track. His vague thought had been that the cardboard boxes would provide sufficient concealment if they should stop at any time and look inside. But examining them again by the light of his torch he realized it was hopeless, there weren't enough of them. He just had to hope for the best.

When the van reached what he was sure was the crossroads junction at the foot of the hill below Mersac, it stopped. Both Françoise and Saul got out; straining his ears Venniker thought he could hear them speaking to a third person, a man. But he wasn't absolutely sure. Then they returned and the journey started again. When they hit the N20, Saul swung left. So they were going north, towards Cahors.

By the time Venniker reckoned they had reached the outskirts of the town, a hint of dawn was showing through a crack at the top of the loading doors. Five minutes later the van came to a halt and the engine was switched off.

Neither Françoise nor Saul got out this time. The only sound was of a match being struck. The scent of a Disque Bleu found its way into the rear compartment. Eventually Saul spoke, his voice surprisingly loud as though behind matchboard not steel. 'I can take you to the station. Why should you walk?'

'I prefer it. Better for us to separate here.'

'At least you'll be in more comfort on the train than I will. I'm not looking forward to driving this tin can back.'

'We should get a better one.'

'I'll look round tomorrow. It's not too late.'

There was a silence. Then Françoise said, 'You haven't said what you think of the store.'

'The store itself is all right. So is the location.'

'But ...?'

'I don't particularly like Venniker. I think he is too inquisitive. And I should have preferred somewhere totally under our control. Your choice of his place was for the wrong reasons. Irrelevant reasons.'

'Nevertheless, it is my choice.' Her voice was very level.

'If you hadn't discovered Venniker happened to live in exactly this part of France, you would have taken somewhere more convenient – near Paris.'

'It wouldn't necessarily have been as safe.'

'Nevertheless being sentimental about coincidence is not amusing. The coincidence itself may amuse. But we are not in this for amusement or sentiment.'

Françoise said, 'You have no sense of history. Which is unfortunate for you. Because an awareness of the past would give you strength for what we have to do in the present.'

Venniker heard the German grunt. He wasn't impressed, whatever the point was that Françoise was making.

Eventually the German spoke again. 'I don't want to argue. What's done is done. As always I accept your decisions – you know that. Maybe it will be all right. I would just like to propose one thing. I am not challenging your leadership, I am asking for your agreement.'

'To what?'

'To my making some inquiries about Venniker, getting another line on him.'

'How will you do that?'

'Through some people back in Germany. It will be quite secure. Their facilities for checking are very good.'

She was hesitating. 'As long as they are told nothing – absolutely nothing – about HANGMAN ...'

126

'Of course.'

'Go ahead then.'

It was a curious relationship, intimate yet cool; one in which Françoise was determined to maintain the dominant position and Saul was apparently content to play up to that – although he seemed no less strong-minded than she was.

Françoise said, 'In perhaps two hours we could know the news from England.'

'It's possible.'

'We ought to be there ourselves.'

Saul replied with something Venniker could not catch. Then he said, 'In any case they are professionals at the game – I guarantee that. If you could have met them you would know it had been for the best, to leave it in their hands. Both from the point of view of efficiency *and* security.'

After a while Françoise said, 'Anyway it will be the real beginning. Everything else has been fundamentally trivial. Now we start.'

The German coughed and Venniker heard a window being wound down. 'We could have coffee at that café over there – it's just opening. There would be no risk.'

'No. I'll leave you now. Drive carefully and time the journey again. I'll telephone you tonight as usual.' The passenger door opened and closed; Françoise had gone.

More time passed. Saul smoked another Disque Bleu. Eventually he switched a radio on. Music was rejected in favour of a news bulletin but even that apparently proved uninteresting. Before it was finished Saul had shifted his tuning until he reached a point where he seemed to be picking up nothing but static. Increasing the volume until the sound became a penetrating hiss, he grunted and settled back to enjoy it.

By Venniker's watch it was now seven-fifty. He wanted to stretch his limbs but was apprehensive of risking the slightest movement so near to Saul. Another twenty-five minutes went by. It seemed incredible that Saul could sit patiently with that relentless hiss for company. Outside the van cars and trucks were going by in increasing numbers.

Suddenly through the hiss a different noise broke, four long pips, repeated over and over again. Within seconds of the pips beginning Saul switched on the engine and swung the van out into the traffic.

Only once did he take what was obviously the wrong direction; the signal began to die away. Venniker heard him curse, the van turned through ninety degrees or more and the course was set again. The signal became louder at once and Saul was hesitating hardly at all at road junctions. The pips stopped as abruptly as the journey had begun. Saul switched off the radio and got out of the van; Venniker heard his footsteps moving away over gravel.

When the footsteps had faded Venniker cautiously opened the doors, revealing a stone wall, a line of trees, finally, in the distance, a bridge with triple towers that allowed for no misjudgements as to his whereabouts. He was in the south west corner of Cahors, on the *quai* leading to the Pont Valentre.

He stepped quickly out of the van and looked round the side. The German was still walking; crossing the *quai*, he went to lean on the stone wall above the river and lit what was apparently his last Disque Bleu since he threw the packaging down into the water. He appeared like a man totally at a loose end, gazing at the river. At first Venniker thought the signal must have come from down there. But then, out of a black saloon parked fifty metres further up the *quai* from where Saul stood, another man appeared. The newcomer was a thickset figure, losing hair, it seemed, from the shine on his forehead; his dark suit looked a little heavy for Cahors in July. Pausing to glance up with elaborate appreciation at the blue sky, he strolled across the *quai* to lean on the wall next to Saul. The other didn't even lift or turn his head. Both stayed motionless, as if engrossed in some passing event of river life.

At any moment, Venniker told himself, Saul would look back and see him. He had to retreat fast. The black saloon was almost too far away for him to read the licence plate but eventually he got it and turned about, muttering the figures into his memory.

As he walked down towards the Pont Valentre, the worst moment of all loomed up. Another car was parked with its nose towards him; he could see the outline of a head in the front seat. If the car had been there to protect the clandestine meeting between Saul and the thickset stranger, Venniker had certainly been spotted getting out of the back of the van. As he drew level with the car he forced himself to glance inside. The head had not turned from its original position above the steering wheel. It belonged to a lean loose-lipped boxer dog, sitting erect with the vigilance of a large animal, with a car to guard and a human being adrift in the world outside. On the whole that seemed to be the extent of its responsibility.

Elated, Venniker risked a glance backwards as he turned away from the bridge into the rue President Wilson. Saul and his companion were still at the same point on the wall. The early morning sun was kissing both their heads.

15

The local bus dropped Venniker in the main square of Mersac at mid-day. Looking up at the scarlet of geraniums spilling from the balcony of the Hotel du Midi, he told himself that he had earned the 18 francs lunch and a bottle of something better than Cahors wine to go with it.

The gendarme was coming out of his cobbled yard. Venniker raised a hand. 'Let me buy you a drink.'

Jules consulted his wristwatch. In the house next to the Agricultural Co-operative, where ceramic tiled steps climbed to a verandah of multi-coloured paving personally designed by himself, mother would be waiting; more than that, the frying-pan would be waiting to bring to the boil onion and garlic and the spoonful of casserole, to transform everything else into odorous life at the exact moment the gendarme crossed the threshold.

'You will forgive me if I leave in five minutes?' Jules said.

'Of course.'

'A beer would be very agreeable.'

At the café next to the pâtisserie Venniker ordered Kronenbergs. 'You were looking for me the other day.'

'I had not seen you since you had a visitor from London.'

'No.'

'He called on me. To ask the way.' The gendarme lit a cigarette. 'He had some business for you?'

'Yes, I had to make a trip to Brussels.'

'I hope it was successful.'

'On the whole.' Impossible to gauge how much Seagram had told him, or whether the visit had been the subject of advance warning from Cahors or Paris. On balance it seemed unlikely he knew much, if anything. Yet.

'There may be some developments this end,' Venniker said.

'Of interest to me?'

'If so, I'm sure you will be told.'

'Good.' The gendarme tapped his cigarette ash into a flower pot. He said it again with the faintest hint of warning in his voice. 'Very good!'

The old woman who helped at the *épicerie* emerged, locked the door behind her and went off in the direction of the bridge. Nothing else was moving in the square; it sweltered lifeless in the heat of noon. Venniker thought of the dining-room with its checker board floor and looped curtains, the slightly sour taste of bread on the tongue before sampling the wine, then, perhaps, Madame's *caneton aux poivres*. He was aware of being very hungry. He said, 'I would like to ask you a favour. In Cahors this morning there was a car – the driver interested me. I have the licence plate number. Could you tell me who the registered owner is if I gave it to you?'

The other looked him in the eyes. 'Perhaps. Was there an accident?'

'Nothing like that. It was just ... odd.'

'Odd?'

'That's all.'

'I may be able to help – unofficially.'

'Thank you.'

Jules watched Venniker write the number on a page of his diary. Without examining it, he slipped it into his cigarette-case and drained his glass. 'I hear you are by yourself again.'

'Yes.'

'You should get a dog.'

An image of the boxer dog behind the steering wheel came into his mind. He smiled. 'Really?'

'Isn't it the way of life of the English country gentleman – the shot-gun and the spaniel?'

'I was never a country gentleman. You must have realized that by now.'

'How would you describe yourself?'

He swirled the dregs of the beer. 'I don't quite know. I was rather mobile – difficult to categorize. An outsider mostly.'

'You say "was". I meant now.'

He grinned, 'Certainly an outsider now.'

131

'So – no spaniel?'

'You've been watching television documentaries about the British, Jules.'

The gendarme put on a martyred expression. 'When there is television in my mother's house you may expect the revolution.' He went off to her, lengthening his stride because he was late. Law and order would have to wait for a couple of hours in the same way the Angelus had waited on mother's other commitments in the village down the road where she had rung it when he was a boy.

At the hotel Madame greeted him. 'No Eloise today?' he asked.

'She is at the clinic in Cahors. For her weight.'

He made sympathetic noises but she was immune to charm until he specified the 18 francs menu and a bottle of the best Bordeaux. Laying the table, she said, 'I hear you are by yourself again.'

'That's true.'

'Then you must take care and eat.' So that was all right.

Back at Larche, limp and perspiring from the ride on a borrowed bicycle after a doze in the hotel to digest the meal, he stopped by the *pigeonnier* and inspected the padlock Françoise had fitted on the cellar door. He saw at once it was too good for him to have any chance of picking it; not that he had any reason to do so since there was presumably nothing inside. In the cool of the gatehouse bedroom he lay down to review the position. A load of explosives or drugs, or both, was obviously going to arrive very soon unless the inquiries the German, Saul, had spoken about to Françoise produced something to make them suspicious. From that moment he would be a party to criminal activity here in France. Jules obviously hadn't been given the story by Seagram or anybody else. There was no sign that anybody in the French police had the slightest idea what was in the wind. It was an impossible state to be left in and there was only one answer: Seagram had got to come over – now. He and the French police could arrange an ambush for Françoise and Saul, grabbing them in the act of unloading the goods. As for other members of HANGMAN, there would surely be enough clues from the ambush for them to be tracked down.

There was a delay of two hours on calls to London but he finally got through and demanded Seagram. He was in a conference and sounded harassed when he came to the phone. 'Who is this?'

'Paul Venniker. Why the hell haven't you been to see me yet? I've been expecting you every day.'

'I'm sorry but I only got clearance this morning.'

'You're too late for the first visit anyway.'

'*Too late?*'

'Yes. But you're lucky – it was a dry run. They came last night and said they'll be back with a genuine load in a few days' time.'

'When you say "they" . . .'

'Françoise and a tough-looking German whom I'd actually seen with her in the Café Grand' Place in Brussels although they pretended not to be together at that time. She called him Saul but it's just a cover name like hers – I'm not sure she didn't invent it on the spur of the moment.'

Seagram was shouting to somebody at the other end; it sounded as though he was trying to do several things at once. Venniker said, 'Did you get that?'

'Yes, sorry . . . you say there's no definite date . . . ?'

'No, they're going to telephone shortly before they arrive. If it's like last night, there'll be barely half an hour's notice.'

Seagram said, 'All I'm waiting for is one call from Paris and I'm on my way. I was on the point of telephoning you. But the last few hours have been pretty hectic, as you can imagine.'

'Why?'

'You haven't heard any news bulletins?'

'I never listen – why do you think I came here in the first place?'

'Your friends have hit the big time. Between nine and ten o'clock this morning two people were assassinated. One was the Leader of the Opposition. The other was a property dealer whom you may not have heard of in your country retreat but who happens to be the biggest slum landlord in England. Both men were shot by marksmen who disappeared into thin air afterwards.'

'But are you sure HANGMAN were behind this – I thought they took care *not* to kill people?'

'A phone call claiming responsibility and giving the correct code words was made to the Press Association within three minutes of the second killing. The message said, "The People have begun the task of cleaning out the exploiters and murderers." There's no doubt about it – it's your friends all right.'

'I see.' He thought of Françoise making love to him in the Brussels bedroom, making him whole again, after the American agent, Ebner, had been blown to pieces. Death in one hand, life in the other. All you had to do was know which hand.

Seagram said, 'They added, if you're interested, that they don't intend to stop until "the capitalist élite and their willing tools have been eliminated".'

'That includes you.'

'I suppose so.'

So this was the news from England, the real beginning Françoise had spoken about to the German in the front of the van a few hours ago.

'If I telephone you in an hour or so, will you still be able to speak freely?' Seagram asked.

'Why not?'

'I meant – will you be alone? The Rayner girl . . .'

'She's gone. You seem to be the only person who doesn't know that.'

'Ah.' He could sense Seagram wrestling with a choice of remarks and then abandoning it as too difficult. 'Well, I'll call back very soon.'

'Before you go, did you get my letter?'

'Yes, thank you.'

'What did you discover about that cottage in Sussex?'

'Well, for a start, the purchaser was a retired police officer. A pillar of the force, they say in Dorset, where he comes from. He makes his own beer and you won't be surprised to hear he stores it in the bloody cellar. The local constabulary who've already sampled it say it's very good.'

'What about other people who were interested in buying the cottage?'

'We're making what use we can of the estate agent's file. There was a man who drove a car with a French registration plate. He sounds the most interesting.'

It was nearly midnight when Seagram called back. 'All fixed. I'm coming via Paris. To save time, can you meet me in Cahors?'

'When?'

'I'm told I can make it by noon tomorrow.'

'There's a bar called Jaime which is almost opposite the Tourist Office. I'll wait for you at one of the tables there.' Venniker looked through the window at the peacocks dozing under the chestnut tree. 'Bring a lightweight suit this time – it's still hot.'

Ten minutes later, coming up from having a shower in the dry-stone hut, he heard the phone again. 'You're certainly working overtime now,' he said. But it was Opal's voice.

'Did I get you out of bed?'

'As it happens – no.'

'Are you still . . . by yourself?'

'Yes.'

'I thought you might be.'

'Well, that's got *that* out of the way,' he said. He picked up the towel he had been carrying, rubbed his head and inspected the result. There seemed to be enough hair there to make a small bird's nest. 'Is Mr Daye back in residence yet?'

'He was here for a while. He left again today for some other deal up north. But he's also fixed one for me. He's shown something I designed to a man who wants to see more. I have to produce a set of designs for his next trip to Paris. Meanwhile he's found me an apartment in Nice. I moved in today.'

He wondered whether to ask her who had paid the advance rent but there didn't seem to be any point.

'Admit you were wrong.'

'Why should I?'

'He owes me nothing. I've given him nothing. But he did that for me.'

He hit the wall with the end of the towel and got a sleeping fly. 'I prefer to believe his publicity. Don't try confusing me with facts.'

Her laugh was strained. 'You *sound* all right anyway.'

Am I that twisted, he thought, that when she's given her chance to do what she's always wanted, something that could pull her into a real existence away from fantasy-hunting, I resent it? 'Good luck anyway,' he said.

'When are you going to visit me in my apartment,' Opal asked. 'It's a bit primitive but there's a real lavatory along the hall – you might enjoy the change.'

'I'll get down one day.'

'On the other hand . . .' she said.

'What?'

'I could come and see you.'

'You could do that.'

'Would that be . . . out of line with what you feel about us?'

The corpse of the fly had remained stuck to the wall. 'There's a problem at the moment.'

'What sort of a problem?'

'It's rather complicated. It would be better if you stayed away.'

She didn't say anything.

'Just for a while,' he said. 'Give me your address, though.'

The silence was long enough for him to imagine her expression, the way she was holding the phone to her ear, the fingers of the other hand plucking at something in that quick nervous way she had.

'Give me your address,' he said again.

'I'll put it on a postcard. Maybe.'

He began. 'This isn't any easier for me than . . .'

'Christ,' she said. 'Oh, Christ! So I have to be sorry about that!'

'I didn't say that.'

'Good-bye, Paul.'

She was gone before he could say another word.

16

Seagram had already arrived at the bar by the time Venniker drove up. This time he was obediently clad in a cinnamon-coloured lightweight. He ordered beer and looked about him like a man who had seen too many places lately. 'What goes on in this town?'

'Not a lot. Comfortable and rather dull. It's a gateway to the south – in summer the British go sweating through in their Maxis bound for the Costa Brava, etc. There's an interesting bridge you ought to look at.'

'Not if I can help it.'

'Lost any more politicians since we spoke?'

'When I left last night, they were all still there, yapping away.' His temper was on a short fuse. 'Let's go over what's happened at your end.'

Venniker described the two visits he'd had at Larche and Saul's meeting with the unknown man near the Pont Valentre. Seagram took the registration number. 'You're sure about the radio signals?'

Venniker called for more beer. 'Yes. They must be quite sophisticated technically. You remember Françoise said she was monitoring the conversation I had with Jewkes in the Café Grand' Place – I thought she was shooting a line then. But it doesn't look like it now.'

Seagram said sourly, 'They're efficient all right. We have two neat corpses now to testify to that.'

'Three – you've forgotten Ebner. Incidentally there was a story about him in one of the newspapers here. How he'd once been a Weatherman in the United States and had disappeared after some bombings in New York in which all the others involved were arrested. I thought that was a pretty good indication he'd been a police agent. Have the Americans acknowledged he was working for them when he was killed?'

'There'd be no sense in their doing so.'

'They don't know about me?'

'No,' said Seagram. He flicked a paper pellet from the table. 'Not through the Yard anyway.'

'What about the Belgian police?'

'Not yet. Leave it to us.'

He persisted, sensing the knots begin to grow again in his stomach. 'How can I feel safe until you've squared my position with them all?' It sounded cowardly. He didn't like the idea that Seagram might think that too.

'You have to trust me. Have I let you down yet?'

He stared into Seagram's eyes, then shrugged letting it go because there was really no other way. 'All right. So what's your plan now?'

'It still has to be worked out locally. At this morning's meeting in Paris the French were arguing against arresting your friends when they arrive. They want to follow them afterwards since it sounds as though the explosives are being collected somewhere near Paris; from their point of view almost the most important thing is to locate the supplier.'

'I should have thought that was taking too much of a chance – following them all the way back to Paris.'

'I'm not mad about the idea myself. Anyway I have an appointment at three thirty with the local coppers. One of the people in Paris came down with me today. He'll be there as well. At the moment he's off having lunch with them.'

'Have you heard how Sir Miles Landon reacted when he was told what his daughter was organizing?'

'He'll learn the facts today. An invitation to come across went to Brussels yesterday morning. The Home Secretary is going to tell him over a drink at the Athenaeum.' Seagram wiped his lips with the back of his hand. 'An affair between gentlemen, you understand – no vulgar coppers about. There's a slender chance he'll be able to say where she's living but I doubt it. Anyway we shan't need his help if we pick her up at your place. There'll be a tap on your phone by tonight so we'll get warning when she's on the way.'

'They could change their minds about how they contact me.'

'If they do, we'll have to rely on your telephoning us. I'm

not sure yet whether the operational headquarters will be here in Cahors or closer to you but you'll be given a number to ring.'

The roofs of the cars in the parking lot opposite the Tourist Office shimmered in the heat. Venniker sat back with his drink. Perhaps this was where the van had been while he crouched in the rear, listening to Françoise and Saul talking. Was that only yesterday morning? 'So I'm not wanted at this meeting of yours this afternoon?'

'No. Do you mind?'

'Hardly. But I rather wondered why.'

Seagram said, 'You're my agent, not theirs – I don't intend to encourage them to get wrong ideas. And I can best protect your position this way.' He looked at his watch. 'I'll have to go now. I've brought over a sergeant with me, Sergeant Bell. Whenever I'm not available on the number you'll be given, he'll be there. Don't be fobbed off with anybody else.'

'Any more on the Frenchman who was interested in the cottage in Sussex?'

'We believe we've identified the car from Channel Ferry records – it was a yellow Porsche. The girl in the estate agent's office came up with a good description of the man driving it. She took him round the cottage herself and he spent as much time in the cellar as in the rest of the accommodation. Finally he said the position wasn't quite right. He gave no name but the girl described him as dark and dishy – he left his mark there. The French are trying to identify him now.'

Seagram watched a girl in a lemon dress go by, and then mopped his forehead. He didn't really seem any cooler on this occasion than on his last visit, despite the lightweight suit. He was a man who decided from the start whether a place was going to make him hot or not, and that was that. 'One interesting thing I meant to tell you ... Do you remember my saying that the Bomb Squad had got some gelignite that didn't go off at Lord Bayes's house? That it was stamped with the name of the factory in France and the date of manufacture? This morning the French police said we'd got it all wrong. According to the factory owners who've presumably produced their records for inspection *no gelignite at all was manufactured on the date we'd given them.*

'Bell rang the Yard from Paris while we were still in the meeting to find out what had gone wrong. The date was exactly as we had said. There was no mistake.'

'*No* mistake?'

'None.'

Venniker laughed. 'Forged gelignite!'

Seagram said, 'You've produced most of the answers so far. See what you make of that.'

Ten minutes later, making nothing of it, not even caring much, Venniker caught sight of Eloise at the bus stop as he reversed out of the parking lot. After he had sounded the horn several times, she woke from an upright doze to accept his offer of a lift back to Mersac. She was carrying a few things from the Prisunic which wouldn't by themselves have warranted the expedition to Cahors. So presumably the weight problem was still being treated there.

They had turned off the N20 when Eloise asked, 'Who was your visitor?'

He frowned. But after all, she might have noticed him outside the bar with Seagram. 'Do you mean the same man I had dinner with?'

'No, not the Englishman. This one was French. Very dark. Handsome.' She looked wicked, stroking the air.

'When was this?'

'The night before last. He was asking where Larche was. He seemed to know your name well.'

'Did he stay at the hotel?'

'No, he had a meal and then left. I think he came from Paris.'

He chewed his cheek, remembering the voice, half-heard, when the van had stopped at the crossroads outside Mersac and Françoise and Saul had got out to talk to someone. 'Why do you think he came from Paris?'

'His voice, his accent.' Eloise looked at him, almost coy. 'Who is he?'

'I don't know. He never arrived. Not to my knowledge anyway.'

Whoever it was must have been making a reconnaissance ahead of Françoise and Saul. Perhaps he had even prowled round Larche, peered through the windows, kept a look-out where the track joined the road to Mersac. That was what Françoise had meant when she had spoken of other arrangements.

Before he dropped Eloise at the Hotel du Midi he said, 'This man – did you notice what sort of a car he was driving?'

She grimaced, concentrating. 'Yellow, I think. Yes, yellow.'

'A Porsche – was that the make of the car?'

She laughed. 'Do you expect me to know everything?'

He went round to open the passenger's door for her, lifting his eyes for a decorous ten seconds in the general direction of the *pâtisserie* while she manoeuvred to prise herself out of the seat. She and a girl in an estate agent's office in Sussex who would have nothing else in common with Eloise, had shared at least this: a visitor in a yellow car who was dark and dishy. And perhaps a cool hand with gelignite as well.

In the evening Seagram arrived unheralded, in clouds of dust that spurted from the wheels of an official-looking Peugeot. There were three French plain clothes policemen with him. While he greeted Venniker, they stood slightly to the rear; then one of them came forward to join Seagram, a small wiry man with black hair in brilliantined waves and eyes so pouched beneath they seemed to be suspended in a floating base, *eau de vie* at a guess. Seagram said, 'This is Commissaire Cuquel from Cahors. He would like to hear your story for himself.'

It took half an hour, going over all the same ground he had covered with Seagram earlier in the day, but this time in French. Seagram sat stony-faced in a corner of the kitchen; he was obviously not understanding more than a tenth of what was said. The Commissaire listened with a faintly exhausted air and only moderate politeness; but when it came to questions at the end he sharpened, walking up and down briskly as he asked them, particularizing points with a forefinger, occasionally pausing to nod to Seagram as though to indicate that, although he'd no doubt done his best, this was what eliciting facts was all about.

Finally he was done. He was about to turn away when one of the others said, 'Should we perhaps deal with the question of observation posts now?' He spoke quietly, a spare, very upright figure in a blue suit that was better cut than any of the others on view; from gazing through the window during the interrogation, he had made a slow, faintly theatrical pivot towards Cuquel.

Cuquel said, 'I shall arrange for a reconnaisance tomorrow morning. Monsieur Venniker will no doubt be available to co-operate then.' He was not going to be rushed.

'Ah, forgive me.' The other man gave an elaborate nod. 'That will be admirable.' The politeness had an edge to it. He was putting down some mysterious marker. Seagram was watching him with a jaundiced interest; the man had switched his gaze again, this time to the John Leech. He was distancing himself from everyone else in the room.

Cuquel seemed unmoved. He said magisterially, 'You will please memorize the following telephone number by which you will be able to contact Superintendent Seagram or his sergeant at all times.'

It was a Cahors number: so they were not setting up a local headquarters. Venniker said, 'Will the gendarme in Mersac know what is happening?'

'Why do you ask?'

'I should not like him to discover there had been something going on in his area without him being told of it. He's been a good friend to me in the past.'

Cuquel shrugged. 'This is a matter that need not concern you, Monsieur Venniker. The gendarme in Mersac will be informed if and when it becomes necessary.' His way of speaking was declamatory, so that any response seemed pointless, otiose. 'Meanwhile we need not trouble you further for the moment.'

Seagram hung back while the others went out of the kitchen door. 'You've got that telephone number straight . . .'

'Yes. I hope you're enjoying co-operation with Commissaire Cuquel.'

Seagram grunted.

'What's his relationship with the man in the blue suit who talked about observation posts?'

'Fairly cool. He's the one who came down from Paris with me. His name's Labarthe. They haven't troubled to explain exactly what his angle is. I thought he was going to smooth my liaison path but it certainly isn't working out like that.'

The others were already sitting in the car. 'However, I've got to play ball with them, there's no choice. The arrest will be Cuquel's show. I just have to hope he doesn't muff things.' Seagram went off morosely. Sweat was darkening the back of his suit.

Next morning Venniker was putting his laundry out to dry on the château terrace when the reconnaissance party appeared down the track. There were seven of them, some in uniform; they must have left their transport near the road. They explored the terrain round the barn and the *pigeonnier* before passing on towards the apricot trees. Nobody bothered to approach him. He thought: all right, to hell with you.

Almost a week passed, with only a visit from Seagram on the third day to provide a diversion. Back in England, Seagram had learned from his daily contact on the phone with the Yard, a political row was raging. HANGMAN was a household word. Members of Parliament had called for extra police protection and the Prime Minister had called for calm and public support for the police. There was talk of a State funeral for the Leader of the Opposition.

Seagram brought his sergeant with him, a red-faced boy from Acton who drank no wine, only beer, and asked for peacock feathers for his girl friend. Although impatient, Seagram was now prepared, it seemed, to give Cuquel's efficiency the benefit of the doubt. Three observation posts had been set up in the grounds and were manned from seven at night until five the following morning. The telephone was tested daily. Once Cuquel spoke on the line, recommending alertness. There was a general sense of occasion all round.

By the following Sunday the occasion was losing its charm. The searing summer wind from the Atlantic, the *autan*, had begun to blow the previous day and when Seagram telephoned in the evening the cumulus was stacking high. 'Anything?' he asked.

'Nothing.'

Seagram cursed.

'Perhaps you'll have a lead from the Brussels end first.'

'I doubt it. There's no news of the girl. The Sûreté have Jewkes under observation but he hasn't met anybody of the slightest interest. Meanwhile, I'm getting daily requests from the

Commissioner for something to give the Home Secretary. He's taking a lot of punishment in the House of Commons over the assassinations.'

'I'm sorry.' He had the vague sensation he was in some way to blame.

'Cuquel claims he can't afford the resources for the observation posts much longer. There are a couple of murders north of Cahors which are not getting investigated fast enough.'

'Perhaps Saul's inquiries about me turned up some item they didn't like and they've decided to drop the whole thing.'

He couldn't hear Seagram's reply. 'Why don't you retire now?' he said. 'I offered you a job – remember?'

In the late afternoon of the following day, the clouds finally released a downpour. The wind had almost spent itself; but with the rain came something else, less agreeable, an ominously fast drop in temperature. Seagram telephoned, glum-voiced, at five o'clock: the observation posts were not coming back to sit through a wet night.

'You're giving up then?'

'Who said anything about giving up? The telephone tap's still running. But I can't tell Cuquel what to do with his own resources.'

'What does the man from Paris – Labarthe – say?'

'He doesn't look too pleased. Cuquel gave the orders when he was away this afternoon. They've just gone into one of their private conferences.'

'Françoise and the German may have gone to England, have you thought of that?'

'If so, they'll be back. She'll want to see your pretty face again.' Seagram was trying to sound confident.

'I wouldn't bank on it.'

Suddenly he became aware of the change in the noise of the rain and swore.

'What's the matter?' asked Seagram.

'There's hail mixed up in the rain. If it goes on that's *finis* to all the bloody crops round these parts. Including my apricots.'

Their farewells were perfunctory. Venniker went out to look at the apricots. It was impossible to know yet whether the damage was going to be fatal. The hail was still coming down. He could cut his throat now or wait a few days. He stared at the white carpet spreading out between the trees and returned to the gatehouse to open a bottle of brandy.

He had eaten and then gone back to the brandy, to nerve himself for the main story in *La Dépêche du Midi* – two and a half columns under the headline *Pour Protéger sa Mère un Enfant Estropié de 10 ans tue son Père de neuf Coups de Carbine* – when the kitchen door opened.

It was Françoise, dressed as before in her black outfit. Round her waist was a belt with a holster on one side and a bullet pouch on the other. He stared in astonishment. 'Are you making the delivery *tonight*?'

'Yes.'

'But there's been no message from you.'

'We decided against it.'

He shook his head, still unwilling to accept it. 'How could you be sure the coast was clear?'

'Someone came ahead. We got the all-clear from him a couple of hours ago that you were home and had no visitors.' She nodded towards the window. 'He's on watch out there. If he sees or hears anything odd he'll signal us with a bleeper.' She took the tube from a breast pocket and held it up. She was enjoying his surprise.

So they had followed the same routine as last time. Either the man Eloise had found so handsome, or someone else, had done a reconnaissance. He made himself smile. 'Well . . . marvellous to see you. How's our Kraut friend, Saul?'

'All right.'

'He's doing the donkey-work in the *pigeonnier*, is he?'

She didn't answer him directly. 'We've completed most of the unloading.' She moved closer to him; she was very pleased with herself. 'Can I rely on you to get me to Cahors by eight o'clock tomorrow morning?'

'But what about your friend?'

'He knows I'm staying. He'll leave separately when he's finished in the *pigeonnier*.'

He nodded, still adjusting to disaster. She raised her eyes to his face.

'You don't object to my staying?'

Everything was going wrong – no telephone warning for Cuquel's people to overhear, observation posts abandoned, and now, it seemed, no chance of getting a message to Seagram before the delivery was over.

'Well?' Her eyes were on his mouth.

He nodded. 'Fine. Somewhere I have a bottle of champagne I bought last Christmas. Why don't we start with that?'

She shrugged. She had been unbuttoning her shirt. Obviously she thought the champagne was a pretty pointless idea, a decadent piece of foreplay in which she could only just about bring herself to indulge him.

Venniker turned towards a corner of the kitchen and then paused, hand upraised. 'Listen.'

'What?'

'Your chum's calling.'

She went quickly to the door and opened it. 'It was your name being shouted,' he said. 'Perhaps he's leaving already.'

He had her worried. Taking the pistol from its holster, she went out at a run. He watched her until she was swallowed up in darkness then shut the door and went to the telephone. It would take her perhaps thirty seconds to get to the *pigeonnier* and satisfy herself that all was well, another fifteen to return. With luck he would just have time to get a call through to Seagram.

The operator in Mersac answered at once, as though she had been waiting for him. No doubt this was one of the benefits of having one's phone tapped. But when the number Cuquel had given him rang out, there was no response. The seconds ticked by remorselessly. He kicked the wall in frustration. After the twelfth ring he put the receiver down and, cursing, turned to open the door again.

She was already inside the room, her back resting against the wall. The pistol was still in her hand but pointing at him this time.

'Who were you trying to telephone?'

Even running flat out, she couldn't have got to the *pigeonnier* and back in the time. She must have smelled a rat before she was half-way there.

146

'An old friend.'

'At one o'clock in the morning?'

'She works in a disco. In Cahors.' He went on fabricating without any real hope it would convince her. 'It's the best time to get her.'

Françoise shook her head. She was tense and very pale. 'Saul was right when he said he didn't trust you.'

'Really?'

'I was a fool not to have believed him. I shouldn't have been so stupid . . . just because you happened to live here.'

It echoed something he had heard Saul say to her in the van that morning in Cahors, the complaint that Françoise had allowed sentiment to influence her in choosing Larche. Sentiment about *what*?

'Who were you telephoning?' she repeated.

'I've already explained.'

'You were lying. Before we leave here tonight you're going to tell us the truth. You'll tell us exactly what game you've been playing even if we have to rip your guts out to make you talk.' She gestured with the gun. 'We're going to the *pigeonnier* now. And don't try to make a break for it. I guarantee I'll drop you before you get two metres.'

Outside the rain had stopped; a few stars offered a little illumination. Françoise made him walk immediately in front of her. When they hit the gravel path for a few seconds, a peacock called hoarsely. By the junction where the other path led down to the *pigeonnier* the outline of a vehicle loomed; it was a van, rather larger than the one used on the previous visit. As they reached it, Venniker heard Françoise draw breath sharply. 'Wait.'

He looked round and sensed rather than saw that her eyes were fixed on the more distant outline of the barn. The peacock spoke again.

'Now what?' Venniker asked.

'Stay where you are.'

'Your nerves,' he began, but suddenly the night split, fell away; from a point on the main track just beyond the barn, a spotlight had reached out, fixing them where they stood. He heard Françoise gasp. Then she was cursing him. 'You bastard, you *bastard*!'

His brain had frozen. But intuition got its message through. There was one response she *had* to make to what was happening out there. She'd use the gun. And he'd be the one to die.

17

Waiting for the bullet, he clenched his shoulders and found himself thinking again, thinking it was unbearable just to wait. He had to try something, anything.

He threw himself sideways and brought his left arm up against the gun at the same time. A bullet went past his cheek before he heard the actual shot; then something else thumped into his side above the kidneys. He almost shouted, in despair and defeat. But it wasn't another bullet. Fortune had not just nodded towards him but adopted him for the night. Françoise had dropped the gun.

He grabbed for it as it lay gleaming in the wet grass in the light of the spot. Somebody was shouting in French, a command to Françoise and himself to stay still. A car engine was started up.

She made no effort to wrest the gun from him but broke away. The spot swung, trying to follow her as she sprinted down the path to the *pigeonnier*; but she was inside before the light enveloped her again and the door slammed shut.

From behind the spot, a car had come racing towards Venniker. It swung to a halt, slewed across the path down which Françoise had retreated. Moving with surprising speed, a burly figure ran from the car to bend over Venniker. 'All right?' a flat London voice said.

He let Seagram help him up and stood rubbing his shoulder where he had hit the ground. He had been aware of a crunch but everything seemed to be moving normally. 'How the hell did you get here?'

'I'll tell you later – who's with her?'

'I presume it's the German.'

Two more men had dismounted from the car. One was Cuquel, the other a stranger, white-haired and smelling of cologne. The stranger carried a walking stick. He lifted it in the direction of Venniker and glanced at Cuquel, inquiringly.

'Monsieur Venniker,' Cuquel said shortly.

'Ah.' The stranger had lost interest at once. He turned to stare at the *pigeonnier*. Behind him and Cuquel, some uniformed police armed with guns had arrived at the double. The vehicle carrying the spotlight was also moving forward.

'There's a third member of the group about the place,' Venniker said, 'a look-out. If he saw trouble approaching he was supposed to give warning. They've got bleepers. I think some of the police ought to be searching for him.'

Seagram shook his head. 'He was picked up in Mersac a few hours ago. That's why we're here.'

'I still don't understand. *How* did you pick him up?'

'The Frenchman in the yellow Porsche who was interested in buying the smugglers' cottage in Sussex was finally identified as someone the French police had lost sight of after the 1968 student riots in Paris. His name then was Raoul Cordet. Labarthe's organization in Paris apparently got on to him again – he was spotted in the Porsche driving south and was followed. We knew nothing about this in Cahors. He drove down here arriving this afternoon, had a look round your place – the team who were behind him at that point thought he'd actually visited you – then withdrew to Mersac and made a telephone call. When he was returning to his car afterwards he broke into a run. The surveillance team concluded he'd spotted them and moved in to pick him up. That was when Cuquel was first told what was happening on his patch.' Seagram glanced at Cuquel in conversation with the white-haired man; some mildly sympathetic feelings were obviously stirring inside him. 'He's got his problems,' he said charitably.

'So Cordet talked?'

'Not a word – he hasn't opened his mouth. But it was obviously a fair bet he was the man that girl Eloise told you she had seen the day you had the previous visit. We guessed he was on look-out duty again.'

'Couldn't you have warned me?'

'I'm sorry. The whole thing was a hell of a scramble. In the end when it was clear Cordet wasn't going to cough, Cuquel just got together his team and we took off.'

The white-haired man was making authoritative thrusts with

his stick while explaining something to Cuquel. A cashmere scarf hung about his neck. Even allowing for the sharpness of the temperature drop after the rain it seemed rather excessive. 'Who's he?' asked Venniker.

'The Préfet. Apparently he got a call from Paris about the investigation and instructed Cuquel he must be present at any arrests. I'd guess he'd been told by the politicians that they didn't want a cock-up. The result is that he's breathing fairly heavily down Cuquel's neck.'

Seagram reached out and took from Venniker's hand the pistol Françoise had dropped. 'Was this the girl's?'

'Yes.'

He examined it in the headlights of the car. 'One up for Fox,' he said without enthusiasm.

'Fox?'

'Fox was the funny at that meeting with the Home Secretary. According to Fox's office, a lot of weaponry associated with the Baader Meinhof gang in Germany is surfacing in the hands of new terrorist groups. This is a Landmann-Preetz pistol. It was almost a Baader Meinhof trademark.'

Venniker thought of the last glimpse he'd had of Fox, in bowler hat and damson silk tie, gliding purposefully through that doorway in Whitehall to pursue the Permanent Secretary. 'And where does all that get you in relation to HANGMAN?'

'You may well ask. But it's this sort of thing Fox lives for.'

Cuquel joined them. By night the pouches beneath his eyes were marsupial. He looked as though he'd had enough of the Préfet.

'Monsieur le Préfet wishes to be assured that the other exit from the tunnel no longer exists.'

Venniker stared. 'How does he know about that exit? I only discovered it myself by accident.'

The Préfet was advancing on them; he had apparently concluded that after all dignity would not be eroded by direct communication. He addressed Venniker in English. 'The tunnel was used to hide stores and escaped airmen who were trying to get back to England during the last world war. An exit was made for emergencies. It was in the face of the cliff.'

'It isn't there any more. I blocked it with stones when I was clearing the tunnel. The door inside the *pigeonnier* is the only way out.'

The Préfet said, '*Eh bien*.' He chopped the last word off very short. 'So they are really in a trap. I think we should now invite them to come out while they can surrender with dignity.'

Cuquel reached in the back of the car and took out a loud-hailer. He addressed the invitation to the *pigeonnier* in words close to those used by the Préfet; it was his declamatory voice again. When there was no reply he repeated the message twice, getting the cadences better each time. There was total silence at the other end.

Turning, he beckoned two of the armed police over. They moved into the beam of the spotlight. 'I wouldn't ...' Venniker began. But it was too late. The shots came from one of the apertures half-way up the *pigeonnier*, dropping the leading policeman. A second burst smashed the side window of the car in which Seagram and the others had arrived.

Under Cuquel's orders they all withdrew into a patch of shrubbery. The spot was extinguished while the fallen police-man was picked up by his colleagues. More shots came from the *pigeonnier* but the rescue party got away unscathed. In and about the shrubbery Venniker could now distinguish at least another dozen policemen, all armed. He turned to Seagram. 'She's not going to surrender to anybody. I could have told you that.'

Seagram made a gesture of despair. 'They shouldn't have been allowed to walk into that bloody spotlight.' He chewed his cheek.

The white-haired man was bending over the stretcher where the wounded policeman lay. 'How does this Préfet know so much about Larche, do you suppose?' Venniker asked.

'According to Cuquel he was a big Resistance leader in these parts during the war. He had meetings with an S.O.E. group here.'

The policeman had been shot through the neck. He was alive but only just. Seagram said savagely, 'Your bloody Françoise will be able to chalk another one up in the name of the sodding people. But I don't suppose *he'll* get a State funeral.' He walked over to Cuquel who had been speaking on his car radio. 'What's the programme now?' He was only barely managing not to interfere.

'We shall put tear gas through the apertures – I have radioed Cahors for it. It will be here in about half an hour. Meanwhile we wait.'

Seagram opened his mouth to speak but the detonation came in the same moment. Beneath their feet the ground shuddered as though a door had been slammed in the cellars of the world. The first explosion was followed by others, satellite to it, but almost as shattering. In the spotlight beam the *pigeonnier* was erupting with each detonation.

At last a sort of peace came back. Venniker felt breath escaping from his lips. Cuquel shouted, 'Everyone remain where they are.' The Préfet slowly lit a cigarette and fitted it into a holder. More minutes passed. A pall of dust now concealed all that remained of the *pigeonnier*.

Venniker thought of the piles of stone laboriously collected, the mound of cement, the days of work. All gone. It was like losing his own creation, not a ruin he had just patched up. And scattered amongst the rubble, something else he had cherished after a fashion, the body of Gail Landon who had preferred to call herself Françoise.

'Hara-kiri,' said Seagram. 'Not a bad solution.'

Venniker shook his head. 'I don't know about the German but she had too much courage for suicide. Something must have gone wrong in there.' He turned on his heel. 'I'm going to have a drink.'

Sitting at the kitchen table, he said, after a while, 'I know she was a menace. I just don't like her dead.'

'People like her have declared war on us. They're lethal. We've got to catch them, stop them fast. Because it isn't a long march through the institutions they're interested in nowadays, it's a bloody short gallop.' Seagram gestured. 'She would have shot you.'

'I don't have any illusions about that.'

'There you are then.'

He struggled with his emotions. He knew now he had come near to loving her.

'She believed I'd betrayed her. As I had.' He stared into his cognac. 'I can't help admiring her for ...' the word took a while to come to him 'for her *certainty*. Everything was clear cut.' He smiled grimly. 'Apart from which she did me a small personal favour.'

'What favour was that?'

'It's not important. It's irrelevant to all this.' He roused himself and sat up abruptly. 'What about that licence number I gave you – the car in Cahors that was driven by the man who met the German?'

Seagram shook his head. 'No luck. According to Cuquel, Paris found it was a stolen car. The owner had been on holiday abroad and hadn't missed it.'

'It was being used by the thief when I saw it?'

'Presumably.'

'So there's no lead at all to the man who met Saul in Cahors?'

'Unless this boy Cordet can be made to talk. He may break when he hears what's happened here.'

Venniker held out the bottle to Seagram. The shoulder was beginning to twinge now. 'All the same, HANGMAN must be finished.'

'If Fox were here, he'd say, how do you know? How can you be sure there aren't a lot of independent HANGMAN cells scattered through Western Europe? We never caught all the Angry Brigade by a long chalk. Is HANGMAN a more sophisticated off-spring with access to Baader Meinhof weapons and an international rather than a national programme? Are the I.R.A. mixed up in it? Anyway, there are two first-class marksmen loose in England who probably still have some bullets left.'

Seagram drained his glass and rose to his feet. Dawn had crept up outside and neither of them had noticed it. 'Let's find out whether Cuquel's decided it's safe to go into that mess.'

Cuquel was talking on his car radio again. He nodded in answer to Seagram's question. 'Two bodies but burned beyond recognition. It was a miracle they were not blown to pieces – the stone work at the bottom of the steps protected them. Apart from the fact that one is female and the other male one can say little more. The teeth may be a help in identification. Please look if you wish to do so – I do not recommend it.'

Amazingly, the steps that led down to the tunnel had survived the explosions although they were crazed and split. A police photographer was at work. The bodies were close together. One of them had no head. The other was smaller but complete in a fashion. After a while Venniker knew it was Françoise.

The first thin ray of sun had pierced the trees above. He clamped his jaws together to stop himself from gagging. Seagram said gently, 'You'd better look at the head. There's still some hair. See if it's like the German's.'

If he didn't look Seagram would know he was weak-bellied. He gazed down where Seagram was pointing. There was nothing of the face left and the patch of hair that had somehow survived was blackened. 'No,' he said, 'I can't say.' He wanted one thing only, to get away from the smell of burnt flesh, this obscene débris of something that had moved and talked. 'No-one could ...' He stopped, almost shivered. Within the hair he had seen something glint with the delicacy of dew, a bloody dew.

'Well?' said Seagram.

He made himself reach down.

'This isn't the German.'

'Why are you so sure?'

He was trying to absorb the new fact, replaying images in his mind that were suddenly lit in a different way.

He opened his palm. Seagram frowned. 'It looks like a ruby.'

'It is a ruby,' he said.

The Préfet had gone and so had some of the armed police. Cuquel leaned against the side of his car fingering the stubble on his jaw. 'The name means nothing to me.'

Venniker said, 'Five years ago Jay Daye was the most successful and highly-paid star on the British pop scene. He was prosecuted for having heroin. He said the police planted it on him. Whether they did or not he claimed he was being hounded by the Establishment just because it didn't like him. He's supposed to have made a lot more money out of property since he settled here.'

'A wealthy former pop star does not strike me as a likely

member of a terrorist group,' said Cuquel. His voice was sceptical, but he was interested all right.

'I agree. But in fact it all fits. The afternoon I returned from my trip to Brussels and London, I found Daye here. He told me he'd happened to see Opal when he was passing through Mersac and he remembered her from some party or other in Rome where she lived for a time. I doubt if that's true but he persuaded Opal it was. At least I think he did.' He could feel Seagram's eyes on his face. 'Anyway, he came back here with her.

'Obviously it was all staged. Gail Landon – Françoise – must have contacted Daye after meeting me in Brussels to say she liked the sound of Larche but that he'd better take a look and see what he could do about getting rid of Opal. Presumably they wouldn't have risked using my place until she was safely out of the way.'

Cuquel consulted a notebook. 'The girl Opal – she is the drug addict who . . .'

'Former drug addict.'

'I see. And how did Daye get rid of her?'

'It was easy. She was thinking of moving on anyway. Daye suggested that if she stayed at his villa in Cap Ferrat he'd pull some strings – get her work. That's where she went. I called there once. He was away on business. I should think he was quite possibly laying in explosives for HANGMAN. His money would have come in handy for that.'

'Apart from this theory, have you other evidence of a link between Gail Landon and Daye?'

'No. Perhaps they met years ago – at university, for example. They were about the same age. It ought to be checked. Just because Daye became a pop star doesn't mean he wasn't radically inclined.'

'We will check of course.' Cuquel held the ruby between thumb and forefinger for a moment then dropped it into a cellophane envelope. 'You will perhaps be kind enough to ask Scotland Yard to make the necessary inquiries as a matter of urgency.' His eyes had swivelled in their pouches towards Seagram. 'Meanwhile we shall look at his addresses in France.'

'I have one more suggestion,' said Venniker. 'It concerns

the man in the yellow Porsche, Raoul Cordet. Put the ruby in front of him when you get back to Cahors. Just that. Don't say anything.'

Their silence, a frowning one in Seagram's case, almost mistrustful on the part of Cuquel, was gratifying.

'Daye was bi-sexual. When I visited Opal at the villa in Cap Ferrat she told me his favourite partner of the moment was half-French, half-Italian. He was at another of Daye's houses, at Fontainebleau. I saw a photograph of him. My guess is that *he's* Raoul Cordet. I may even have seen him in the flesh without realizing it. When I went into Ebner's apartment house in Brussels I remember a queer standing on the corner of the street. It was too far away for me to recognize the features. I'd gamble what's left of the apricot crop on that having been Cordet keeping watch on my visit to Ebner.'

Cuquel was nodding his head slowly. 'You may be right. Yes, I think so.'

'What's Cordet's history?'

'His full name is Raoul Barres Cordet. Age 26. Father French, mother Sicilian. He came to notice in the riots at the Sorbonne in 1968. He belonged to a group known as the Situationists. I believe the leaders of the Angry Brigade in England picked up their ideas from this group. The Situationists were committed to the destruction of what they called the Spectacle. The Spectacle was their jargon word for the commodity society by which Man was imprisoned. Western Man that is.

'For the proletariat, said the Situationists, life is simply a show, nothing more.' Cuquel paused, looking up at the sun on the clock tower of the gatehouse. 'To which I would think it permissible to reply – "Is it not so for us all?"' With the Préfet out of his hair, he was recovering his form. 'Did Gail Landon – Françoise – ever use the term "the Spectacle" when talking to you?'

'Not that I remember.'

'Or the German she called Saul?'

'No.' Venniker lit a cigarette. 'You said the Situationists *were* committed to certain ideas. Do you mean the group no longer exists?'

'Ah.' Cuquel adopted a martyred expression. 'You must not

ask a simple police officer these questions. You must ask Monsieur Labarthe who comes from Paris and is expert in such movements.' He was about to overplay the irony but the car radio was calling him and he turned to answer it.

Seagram looked grimly at Venniker. 'Another bloody Fox – Labarthe. They'll be tally-hoing together over here before the day's out.'

Cuquel replaced the handset. 'One or two local journalists have arrived but they have been stopped by my men. We shall keep them away for today. However, you will no doubt wish me to organize the arrangements under which you see them in due course?'

'Do I have to see them at all?'

'You will find them difficult to avoid. Unless you disappear altogether. I should be obliged if you would refrain from doing that.' Cuquel rubbed his hands together briskly. He had scented triumph, perhaps fame. 'If you agree, Chief Superintendent, I think we should return to Cahors.'

Venniker stood watching the car drive off. As it disappeared into the orchard, the peacocks appeared from the other side of the barn as though at a signal, moving in cautious arrowhead formation to inspect the night's work. They were calling while they advanced, as though warning him and anyone else present that everything must now be explained and accounted for.

Venniker turned and went into the gatehouse. Sitting down at the kitchen table to finish off the cognac, he found *La Dépêche du Midi* folded as he had left it, at the story of the crippled boy who'd killed Dad to protect Mum. That was it, he thought, normality again, the reassuring, everyday, humdrum stuff.

18

Apart from shaving and taking a shower, he had achieved no more than cooking himself an omelette when Seagram telephoned to say that a police car would pick him up in half an hour.

'What else can I do?' he asked. 'You've got it on a plate. It's up to you and Cuquel now.' But he was pleased all the same.

Seagram said briskly, 'I thought you deserved to be here.' He wouldn't say more.

In Cahors he was driven to the back of police headquarters to avoid a cluster of journalists and photographers. He was met by the red-cheeked Sergeant Bell, triumph gleaming in his eyes. 'Cordet broke an hour ago.'

'The ruby?'

'Yes. He pretended not to understand what it was to begin with. Then he fainted – fell off the chair. It was a doddle after that.'

In the anteroom to Cuquel's office, Seagram also looked elated. He no longer even seemed frustrated by his spectator status. Through the open inner door Cuquel was visible, behaving like a great man, speaking on the telephone with cuff-shooting élan.

'Has Cordet spilled everything?' Venniker asked.

'We think so. He was Daye's boy all right. His pouf-de-luxe you might say.' Seagram grinned; it was going to be his joke for the day obviously. 'Daye seems to have dominated him completely. That's how he found himself in HANGMAN.'

'So he's not political . . .'

'He is and he isn't. He's got all the jargon of course and he likes to think of himself as one of the leaders. He says they'd all made the same analysis – economic and social stress in the

U.K. had reached a point of crisis where a terror campaign would stand a good chance of destabilizing the system beyond recovery. Out of the chaos produced by bombing and assassinating Establishment figures in the name of the People, would come the opportunity for the People to take over.'

'Always assuming "the People" wanted that.'

'The People,' said Seagram, 'would want what HANGMAN told them they ought to want. Anyway, Cordet claims this is why he was in HANGMAN. But Cuquel and I are sure that it was primarily a sex thing – he liked Daye to *use* him – in every way.'

'How did HANGMAN begin?'

Seagram sent Bell out to find some coffee and sat himself on a corner of the desk. 'According to Cordet – who is a rather prejudiced witness but never mind – it really started with Jay Daye. It didn't have a political base then. Not primarily, anyway. Daye was obsessed by the fact that he had been hounded by the Establishment – as he thought. He wanted to get his own back. But how could he do it?

'He came up with the idea that the perfect revenge on an Establishment that had used heroin to destroy him was to give it a taste of its own medicine. It started as a sick joke. He did a certain amount of research to discover where the sons and daughters of the police and the prosecuting lawyers and the judge who convicted him were being educated. Then he decided that was piddling – he'd establish a syndicate that would really push drugs into those areas of British life he hated.'

'I don't believe it – Gail Landon wouldn't have been mixed up with ...' he hesitated, searching for a word that gave her something but not too much ' ... with somebody working out a kink, a revenge fantasy.'

'You'll have to believe it because it's true. Daye, with Cordet's help, contacted criminals in order to get the thing going properly. That's how Jewkes came in – although, along with the other straight crooks, he was kept out of the inner circle and never fully understood what the organization was after. Getting supplies of cocaine and heroin wasn't difficult for a person with Daye's resources. But exporting the stuff safely to England was tricky. They used a motor launch for a time until it was sunk

160

in some accident. Then Daye had a brainwave. He'd seen in a newspaper a photograph of Gail Landon with her father on a trip to England. The caption said she was doing social studies in Brussels. Gail Landon had lived with Daye for a while when they were both at university. She was way out on the Left and he'd been quite radical in those days. So he contacted her and took her into his confidence.'

Bell came back with black coffee in very small cups. Seagram examined them with stoical resignation, then drank his own in one gulp. 'Cordet says he never knew her well although she was once a Situationist like himself. It's obvious he dislikes her – there's a lot of sexual jealousy because of her past relationship with Daye. And he blames her for last night. His version is that Gail Landon was on the look-out for somebody like Daye with enough money to fund her own schemes. To begin with she went along with Daye's private vendetta against the British Establishment and agreed to smuggle heroin into the country, travelling with her father on his trips back. But after a while she persuaded Daye that this was kid's stuff and that they ought to get down to something more serious. According to Cordet, this, she said, was the historical moment, when the Establishment could be destroyed – all that was needed was a determined attack from an entirely new quarter. Daye was at first sceptical and then fascinated. He agreed to cooperate in Gail Landon's scheme and Cordet went along because of Daye. They formed HANGMAN – she thought up the name. There was some special reason behind her choice but Cordet says he never knew it.'

'Did she invent the code names for each of them?'

'Cordet never had one. Daye was always referred to as Serge. And very early on Gail Landon insisted on being known only as Françoise.

'HANGMAN'S first big problem was getting hold of enough explosives. They established that it wouldn't be too difficult arranging for the first publicity bombs to be let off. But how was a regular supply of gelignite and detonators to be obtained?'

'Is that where the German came in?'

'Yes,' said Seagram, 'that's where Saul came in.'

Cuquel had finished his telephone call. He beckoned them into his office and shook Venniker by the hand. Success had extinguished all signs of fatigue in his face. He'd also had a shave. He offered them more coffee. From a chair behind the door, Labarthe rose and greeted them with less zest.

'I was telling Venniker about Cordet's confession,' Seagram said.

Cuquel waved a hand. 'Please continue.'

'Cordet says the German's real name is Franz Leff. He didn't seem to know Françoise called him Saul. Leff was a glamour boy in the Berlin student movement. Gail Landon got hold of him to be the fourth member of HANGMAN, along with Cordet and Daye. They'd apparently met in England in 1968 – he'd come over to be one of the instructors in riot tactics for the Grosvenor Square demonstrations against the Viet Nam war. Cordet admired the German very much. Although Gail Landon still saw herself as the leader, taking all the decisions about the timings and targets for the bombs and about the content of the messages to the press and so on, in Cordet's eyes Franz Leff was the main force. As soon as he joined them he tightened up security and got rid of some of the more unreliable of the criminal support elements. And he obtained the explosives.'

'Does Cordet know where?'

Seagram shook his head. 'None of the others was allowed to be with him when he collected the stuff. It was somewhere in the Paris region. He said it came through his old Baader Meinhof links. It seems probable.'

'Storing it at my place seems pointless – it's further away from England, not nearer.'

Cuquel looked up from a paper he was about to sign. 'The store of explosives they planned to establish at Larche was nothing to do with HANGMAN's operations in England. It was in readiness for a campaign in France. They believed that once England was in panic it would be a good moment to start in France. Later it would be Italy's turn. It must be said that their concept was not parochial.' He smiled sardonically.

Labarthe had lit a small cigar. He lay back with his eyes half-closed, staring out of the window. Venniker followed his gaze. In the square outside the leaves on the trees were stirring. A faint echo of the wind from the Atlantic had returned. Ash and dust would be lifting from the rubble of the *pigeonnier*, the

162

charred scraps of Françoise's black outfit would be twitching on the obscenity that had been her body, if the police hadn't removed it yet.

Venniker tried to shake the image from his mind. 'The cottage in the Sussex village which Cordet looked at . . .'

Seagram interrupted. 'He's talked about that as well. He'd been told that a Cuban Landon knew when she had guerrilla training in South America would be joining HANGMAN soon and would be in charge of a dump in the south of England. The cottage was to be occupied by him.'

'So where do you go from here?'

'The Belgian police are picking up Jewkes – although I doubt if he knows much that will be new to us.'

'And the German?'

'Everybody will be looking for him.'

'There's still the man I saw him meet in Cahors to be identified.'

'We put that to Cordet. He's sure there's no one else who was in the leadership of HANGMAN. There were just the four of them.'

'So who was it?'

'Cordet thought it might have been one of the drugs suppliers.'

Somebody came into the room with a message for Cuquel. He read it and rose to his feet. 'You must forgive me – the Préfet is now free. I have to give him the latest account of what we know.' He went off through the door, Labarthe following silently at his heels.

'Does he ever speak – Labarthe?'

'Not in *my* presence.'

'Perhaps he's just here for the show – the Spectacle.'

Seagram grunted rudely, then smiled. 'I've got one more piece of news that may amuse you. Just before you arrived I heard on the telephone from London that a story had been peddled to a German paper about Sir Miles Landon – that he had been involved in smuggling drugs into England. Apparently the line is that he and some other British officials at E.E.C. headquarters have been using their positions at Berlaymont to run an enormous racket. It hasn't been played by the British press yet – their libel lawyers must be sniffing round it rather cautiously. But it'll come out in some form. Then there'll be a god-awful row.' He didn't look too upset.

'But it's nonsense.'

'Of course.'

'I wonder who put the story out?'

'I suppose it's possible that somebody like Jewkes on the fringe of the business discovered who Françoise was and decided he could make a killing by embroidering on the fact she was Landon's daughter. But I don't buy that altogether – the coincidence with HANGMAN being smashed is too odd.'

Venniker lit a cigarette. 'They were all using each other in different ways, weren't they? Daye used Cordet, Gail Landon used Daye. And the German, Leff – was *he* used or was he using *them*?'

Seagram shrugged his shoulders. 'Everybody uses everybody – that's crime, that's life.' He stood up. 'Let's find a cold beer. Then I'm going back to London to report. If I'm lucky I'll escape before the British press arrive – I hear there are some of them on the way.'

'What's going to be said to the press about me?'

'Nothing specific. Simply that you have given the police all possible help. The trip to Brussels won't be mentioned.'

They sat at the same café where they had met a week before. The breeze had dropped again and the sky looked tranquil. Venniker felt the lack of sleep beginning to prick his eyelids.

'Sorry about the pigeon house,' said Seagram. 'Perhaps you can get compensation under French law.'

'I doubt it.'

'Would you like me to ask Cuquel?'

'Later maybe.'

Seagram examined a torn nail. 'About Opal Rayner ...'

'What about her?'

'I understand that when the local police searched Daye's villa in Cap Ferrat this morning there was no trace of her.'

'She telephoned me the other day to say she was moving out.'

Seagram said, 'Wouldn't you like me to try and trace her for you? With Cuquel's help we ought ...'

'No.'

'I don't believe it does people any good living on their own.'

'She's got to discover how to swim by herself.'

'You want that?'

'Yes I do.' He raised his glass. Seagram was watching him and he took care to look elsewhere. He wasn't sure whether he was irritated or touched. 'All this ought to do you some good in the promotion stakes back at the Yard.'

'If it does, I'll have you to thank.'

'So much for HANGMAN then.'

'Until the next one comes along. It's the phenomenon of the times and we've no real answer to it. Except when somebody like yourself gets inside and tells us what's going on.'

Venniker poured out the remains of his beer. 'I'm still curious why she called it that – HANGMAN. There must be *something* to the name surely? Perhaps the initials stand for some up-and-coming radical movement.'

'If they did stand for anything Fox would have spotted it.' Seagram sighed. 'I'll have to get back. Don't go away from Larche without letting me or Cuquel know where you'll be. I'll be in touch again in a day or so.' He reached out a hand in the same awkward way he had done once before and placed it on Venniker's forearm. 'If the girl came back of her own accord – what would you do then?'

'I don't know.'

Seagram said, 'I see.' He sat back for a moment, thinking something through.

By the time the police car dropped him back at Larche, it was late in the afternoon. The bodies had been taken away from the rubble. Explosive experts were grubbing through the dust for treasure to put in their little plastic bags. None of them looked up as he passed.

Fetching a bottle of wine he took it to the terrace and found a shaded spot. Across the valley he could see the glitter of tourists' cars, moving along the road between the Agricultural Co-operative and the bridge below Mersac. Soon the tide would reach its flood. From Bruges, Berne and Bremerhaven they would come, obediently dropping speed at the foot of the path that afforded the best view of the *donjon* before pressing on to the Michelin rosette at Caldec and the other shrines agreed by the guidebooks to warrant an actual halt. Strident English voices would call among the stubby grey willows that surrounded the swimming pool at the camp site. It would be a time to avoid the hotel and the cafés and to buy bread early in the day.

Aldo came up from behind and stood in the same shade. He was wary but curious. 'The police have finished with you?'

'Yes.'

'Will there be trouble?'

'I may have to give evidence at a trial, I suppose. Nothing else. So far as what happened last night goes, I was acting on their instructions.'

'The police?'

'Yes.'

'You helped them set a trap for those who had the explosives...'

'In a way. It would be best if you didn't talk about it, though.'

Impossible to tell from Aldo's expression what he made of the information; was it a shade unpalatable, such active co-operation with authority? Probably it made no difference as long as trouble stayed away.

Venniker gestured towards the remains of the *pigeonnier*. 'We'll have quite a mess to clear up.'

Aldo shrugged. Clearly he wanted to say – why bother? Nature will take over the rubble as quietly and effectively as it took over the ruins of the château. What's to be achieved by the labour of making it look neat? He went off with his customary casual salute, presumably reassured. Venniker noticed that as he wheeled his bicycle past the explosives experts, conferring by their vehicle, he kept his eyes straight ahead, unwilling even now to risk being thought in any way relevant to what had happened.

Venniker dozed, woke to drink more wine, dozed again. Hunger finally drove him back to the gatehouse and the dis-covery that he had forgotten the need for fresh bread, and, worse, was short of almost everything except eggs. He got the omelette pan out, then decided that if he was going to lay in rations against a siege by the press, now was the time to do it.

He parked the 2CV below the bridge at the foot of the climb to the square in Mersac and walked along the bramble path that provided an unobserved approach to the shops. He was met there with a wide-eyed marvelling, even respect. He had acquired a different status since his last visit. He might not be Quercynois, but he wasn't altogether foreign now; he was something between, a valued notoriety. Like the English who had once come as invaders and had then stayed long enough to be preferred sometimes to the French of the north, he had begun to belong.

He studied the square but could see no obvious journalists hanging about. Walking quickly into the cobbled yard in front of the gendarmerie, he put his head round the door of the office. Jules was writing at his desk; he looked up after a suitable bureaucratic interval. 'They have let you go in Cahors then ...'

'Shouldn't they have done?'

'Everyone is guilty of something. Withholding information can be an offence. Although it seems that only I can complain on that score.' He was being cool.

'I came back to ask you if you'd direct any reporters who come looking for me to take the route to the Grama'.' It was the other way on to the *causse*, where the road petered out and dust took over and there was nothing to find but the bones of sheep under the juniper bushes.

'You do not wish to be famous?'

'I wish to be unfamous.'

'You may find that difficult. Two English reporters have already arrived at the hotel.'

Jules looked down at his papers again. There was a silence between them, a definite coldness. Venniker said, 'I asked that you should be told.'

'Asked whom?'

'A Commissaire from Cahors who came to see me a week ago. His name is Cuquel. Were you told?'

'No.'

'I'm sorry.'

The gendarme shrugged. 'Of course I met your Chief Superintendent friend at the beginning. I knew from him that something was happening.'

'I should have preferred you to know everything.'

'Yes.' Jules was looking at his hands on the desk. Then he spread them quickly. It was an armistice. 'I believe you.' He rooted amongst the papers. 'By the way I have some news for you. About the car.'

Venniker frowned. 'What car?'

'The car which you saw in Cahors. You asked me to find out the name of the owner.'

He snapped his fingers, then hesitated, wondering how much to explain. But it seemed best to be frank now.

'As a matter of fact it doesn't concern me any longer. I mentioned it to my friend from Scotland Yard. He found out the answer.'

'You found it interesting?'

'No, disappointing.'

'Diplomats do not interest you ...?'

'You're talking about the owner?'

'The car was registered in the name of a First Secretary in an Embassy in Paris.' Jules began searching his desk again.

'But it had been stolen.'

'That had not been reported when my inquiry was made.'

'Apparently the owner didn't discover it had gone until several days ...' Venniker broke off, lifting his eyes up to the bougainvillea outside the window, up and up to the sky. Ah!

There could be no proof as to whether or not the car had been stolen by the time he saw it in Cahors – only the word of the owner. Supposing some suspicion had reached the owner, or the Embassy, that it had been seen ...

'An Embassy in Paris, you said.'

'Yes.'

'Would it represent a ... a freedom-fighting, peace-loving country perhaps?'

The gendarme smiled. 'Most peace-loving. The most freedom-fighting, peace-loving of all perhaps.' He held out a piece of paper. 'There is the name of the diplomat.'

Venniker took it.

'So you are interested after all?'

'Yes,' he said. 'Yes indeed.'

He stood up. 'Will you come and have a glass of wine with me at Larche soon?'

'When the others have gone.' He walked to the door with Venniker. 'No more explosives please. We are not used to these things in Mersac. Certainly not for the past thirty years.'

Venniker gazed across the square. 'Were you here when the SS came through – the day they shot people after the German officer had been nailed to the flagpole on the *donjon*?'

'I was here.'

'But you were only a boy . . .'

'I was four. My elder brother was one of those they murdered.'

'It must be difficult to forget something like that.'

'I do not try to forget. We have a duty to remember. That is the least we can do.'

The sun was going down. Venniker paused at the head of the path leading to the 2CV. He felt a reluctance to go back to Larche yet. Turning about he climbed the hill to sit on the grass in front of the *donjon* and eat some of the bread and cooked meat he had bought in Mersac.

Over to his left the stage that had been set up for dancing on Bastille night was still in position. The posters of a pop group, allegedly from St Tropez, were curling from its wooden base; a pile of rubbish stood at one corner.

So now he knew who had met Saul that morning in Cahors; he knew why Franz Leff, alias Saul, had spoken so confidently about checking on himself; he even knew the answer to Seagram's riddle about the gelignite that had been dressed up to appear as though it came from the same source as the explosives used by the Angry Brigade. He knew, much better than Jay Daye and Raoul Cordet who believed they were the leaders of HANGMAN what its true significance had been.

Leff himself would never be caught now, that was certain. His contact in the Embassy would have got him back to safety as soon as the first indication had come that something was going wrong with HANGMAN. Perhaps its true masters had their suspicions aroused when they found some flaw in Venniker's cover story; or rumblings from Brussels might have reached them of what had been said to Landon about his daughter's activities. The leakage to the German newspaper about a drugs smuggling scandal in the European Community Headquarters involving the British was probably the first shot in a campaign to get some propaganda consolation from the wreckage.

A tortoiseshell cat appeared from under the stage and moved ponderously over to investigate Venniker. He placed a piece of the cooked meat on the grass and let the cat share his supper. It was agreeable, to think that he was aware of dimensions to HANGMAN that neither Seagram nor Cuquel suspected. Or did they? Seagram *might* have been dissembling all the time. Somehow he didn't believe that. And the French? What exactly had brought Labarthe hurrying down from Paris to be at Seagram's and Cuquel's elbow throughout? Had the apparent acceptance of the story that the car in Cahors had already been stolen been a little too ready, a piece of play-acting to conceal an awareness of an embarrassing truth?

Anyway, how much the most convenient thing to assume they already knew, or knew enough, about the real backer of HANGMAN. There lay the quickest path to disengagement from the whole affair. Because he wanted to be left alone, to try to recover the peace of mind he had known – not just before Seagram's appearance on a sultry afternoon to remind him of an existence he had tried to forget, but in the days before he had brought Opal Rayner to Larche, thinking they could build a bridge to each other.

Narrowing his eyes, Venniker searched the panorama across the valley for the terrace where he had sat a few hours before. It was easily found, marked at its right-hand corner by a cloud of dust suspended over the spot where Gail Landon had died. Although he had no sensation of grief now, he was left with the knowledge of loss, a void within him. Someone who embodied certainty as she had done, even when violence and death were the end, someone so in command of her destiny, quickened flesh, made stale life vivid again.

But even Gail Landon had after all been duped about her destiny. She had thought of HANGMAN as her own instrument for destroying a society she found intolerable; yet from the moment Franz Leff had joined forces with her and Daye she herself had been the instrument of Leff and those who stood behind him. Everybody uses everybody else, Seagram had said, and that had been the story of all the participants in HANGMAN. Perhaps it was the inevitable fate of ventures like that; sooner or later to wind up being manipulated by others, by madmen, by ambitious politicians, by countries convinced that while history's card might be marked in their favour, it must also be given a helping nudge.

A cyclist was pedalling slowly up the hill on the other side of the valley, towards the ruined cottage that overlooked Mersac. At the crest another appeared from the opposite direction. They raised hands in salute and dismounted, perhaps to talk about the events of the night. It was impossible to recognize them at this distance. Venniker guessed they were *petits cultivateurs* who scratched an existence on the margins of the *causse*. Like Venniker himself, they owed this society nothing. They might not have cared at all if HANGMAN had remained in existence and had shot the rest of the Establishment stags, not only in England but in France as well. Yet this same society had somehow created for him and the cyclists and Seagram and all the other actors in the Spectacle some sense of freedom. And, however much Gail Landon and others like her might say it was illusion, in the end they would find that hard to believe.

Because this freedom (real or imagined) was perhaps in danger, he knew he would have to make sure, however reluctantly, that Seagram knew HANGMAN's true meaning. Even at the risk of having Fox, in bowler hat and damson silk tie, and Labarthe and others like them, descend on Larche. But a letter would do – tomorrow.

One question still nagged. Why had Gail Landon called it HANGMAN? Had it any meaning – or was it like those cryptic announcements on the breasts of tee shirts, like the names of pop groups, a random word taken for its deliberate insignificance? He would have said that nothing was random in her life. Standing with her on the terrace at Larche, he had once felt within reach of learning something that might give the answer to this riddle. Now he would never know.

Rising finally to begin the walk back to the car, he noticed that there was scaffolding near the door of the *donjon*. It could scarcely be part of the paraphernalia for Bastille night – there were also stones and bags of cement alongside. He smiled up at the tower, in disbelief at what the evidence was telling him.

Yet it was true. Someone in an office in Paris had finally taken a pen and had written – the *donjon* at Mersac must not be allowed to crumble away. He stroked its side as he had once stroked the *pigeonnier*. Amazing! He was consumed with a foolish pleasure, as though he had personally campaigned for this.

Something brushed against Venniker's legs. He looked down. It was the tortoiseshell cat. 'What do you think of that?' he said. There were still surprises in the world. Rebuild, they had decided, we will rebuild! He went back down the path. Who would have guessed they would see the point of *that*?

Appendix

From *The Story of Special Operations
Executive in France in World War II*
by Richard Coddington (pp. 278-81)

... In January 1944, another woman became a Circuit Commander.
Barbara Lemoigne, using the field name of *Françoise*, assumed control
of HANGMAN which was operating in the Lot to the north of George
Hiller's FOOTMAN. The daughter of an English mother and a French
father, she had been brought to London as a child and grew up in the
café opened by her parents in Soho.

The event which produced this change in the leadership of HANG-
MAN was the death of Musgrave from pneumonia, a serious loss for
London at a critical time. But with F. J. Bogarde (*Saul*) acting as her
principal assistant and Max Vint (*Serge*) taking over as courier,
Françoise quickly demonstrated remarkable powers of leadership, and
the rail-cutting and other sabotage operations which had gone sluggishly
during Musgrave's illness were pressed forward with renewed vigour.

However, London's satisfaction at now having two successful
Circuits controlled by women (Pearl Witherington's WRESTLER
was still operating in the Indre) soon received a severe jolt. From a
Free French source came news of some negotiations which *Françoise*
had been conducting with Maquis groups in the Lot, negotiations in
which *Françoise* appeared to have adopted a line which went a good
deal beyond even the generous latitude allowed by London to Circuit
Commanders' discretion. According to the French report she had put
it to the Maquis leaders that the defeat of the Germans in France was
to be only the beginning of the real struggle; thereafter it would
be necessary, using the fluid period at the end of the main hostilities
with Germany, to develop a broad-based campaign to overthrow
capitalism – initially in France, then in Britain. We must be ready, if
need be (she was quoted as saying) for another hundred years of war in

173

order to liberate the working-class peoples of Western Europe; reserves of weapons and explosives provided for the immediate campaign against the Germans were to be husbanded with this longer perspective in view.

London was not at first disposed to take the French report too seriously. It had come through de Gaulle's Headquarters and, given the barbed relationship between the General and S.O.E., the possibility that malice had provided the more dramatic detail of the report was canvassed by a good many at Baker Street who preferred to focus their attention on *Françoise*'s achievements in the field.

But doubts grew. The Security Service who were now consulted about Barbara Lemoigne's antecedents (for the first time or not is unclear) came up with the disagreeable information that not only had she a pre-war history of Trotskyist activity but Bogarde (*Saul*) had been her closest political associate at the time. Moreover, it now appeared that she had manoeuvred without letting her own hand show, to get another previous acquaintance, Max Vint (*Serge*) sent to HANGMAN when Musgrave died.

It was decided to summon *Françoise* home for a detailed interrogation. She refused London's order twice, claiming that particular operations already in hand made this impossible. And indeed HANGMAN's performance continued to be most impressive. On May 1st, an important and heavily guarded power station in the north-east of HANGMAN's territory was completely destroyed. The event was sufficiently important for Mr Churchill to be informed personally.

London again hesitated, then came to the conclusion that it would drop Bannister on HANGMAN's headquarters to make a personal investigation. Bannister's plane was due to take off on the night of the 19th May. On the 18th came the news of the disaster which was effectively to destroy the Circuit. *Françoise* had gone to meet *Serge* at an abandoned farm on the *causse*. Entering the yard, she seems to have realized, too late to turn back, that she had failed to check that the all-clear signal was flying. It was not. *Serge*, betrayed by one of his agents, had already been arrested and the Germans were lying in wait for anyone else who might turn up at the farm. It is not clear exactly how the end came for *Françoise* but it seems that she was determined not to be taken alive and fell in an exchange of shots with the German ambush party.

Serge who was badly tortured during his interrogation had given nothing away about *Françoise*; but his answers yielded enough for the Germans to embark on a search for *Saul* with good clues to where he was most likely to be found. However, warning seems to have reached him through the Maquis and he was well away when the Gestapo party arrived at his flat in Rocamadour. *Saul* joined up with a Maquis group and was later killed in one of the attacks on the SS Reich Division as it moved north in June 1945 to oppose the Allied landings in Normandy. A few days after his death, the Division took its inhuman revenge for the incessant guerrilla attacks upon it, first in Veyrelau, then in Mersac and later in the village of Oradour-sur-Glane where it slaughtered the whole population.

One man of the Maquis group joined by *Saul* who survived the war and was to become a distinguished Left-wing lawyer was Boris Guillot. He knew *Françoise* well and recalled her in his book *Au Temps de l'Héroisme*. She was, he said, immovable in her conviction of what must be done, implacable in her determination to employ every means to hand. She had no doubt, according to Guillot, that the complete erasing of the *deux cent* families was a pre-condition for true social justice to prevail in France. And she was supremely contemptuous of arguments, whether they came from Moscow or anywhere else, that the tactics of revolutionary struggle could ever succeed without the gun and the bomb.

As an illustration of the feeling that animated *Françoise*, Guillot recalled the time when she heard in his presence of the deaths in a particularly gruesome road accident of some Frenchwomen, mostly from local *bourgeois* families, who had organized that day a charitable garden party in the grounds of a château made available for the occasion by the German High Command. 'We were drinking wine and she raised her glass silently at the news. Then she turned to me and said, "Now I understand a little better how Léon Bloy felt." When I looked puzzled, she reminded me of an occasion when Bloy was writing of the burning to death of Parisian society women at a charity bazaar, and had spoken of the clear and *delicious* feeling that came to him. Only the small number of victims had set limits to his joy. That word *bazaar* coupled with the word CHARITY! But all the same, at last! AT LAST! Here was a beginning of justice! *Françoise* paused and placed a hand on my arm. "Another beginning, Boris," she said.'

Such was the character of Barbara Lemoigne, one of the most remarkable if short-lived of S.O.E.'s Circuit Commanders. Under her direction HANGMAN possessed a deadliness which the German occupation forces certainly learned to fear. Had she survived, the course of European history might also have borne its marks.